LEE WARREN

The Revelation: A Christmas Novella

The Mercy Inn Series (Book 3)

Chapter 1

D r. Sophia Gibbs was doing everything she could to get off the phone, but her mother was relentless. "I've already told you, Mom. This was just a trip I needed to take for myself."

"But I had the perfect guy picked out for you. He's Marge's son, and he's a trial lawyer. He was looking forward to meeting you before you bailed on Christmas dinner."

"I don't want an arranged marriage, Mom. I've been—"

"Oh, don't be silly. Nobody said anything about marriage. It's just Christmas dinner with a handsome, wealthy, available man. I don't understand why you'd leave Atlanta during the holidays to traipse off to some godforsaken inn in Colorado."

"First, I don't need any help in finding a da—"

"Could've fooled me."

"And second, I chose to come here because—"

"You don't have to explain yourself to me."

Sophia gritted her teeth. Of course she did. That's all her mother seemed to expect her to do. "I have to go. I think I missed my turn." She didn't even feel guilty about lying. She ended the call and tossed her phone into the seat next to her. Her mother made her feel like such a failure for being thirty-eight and never married.

And her older sister, Isabella, was even worse. She married her high school sweetheart shortly after graduating and had three children with him. Isabella could never understand why Sophia chose her career as a family practice doctor over a family—as if she couldn't have both. Sophia couldn't bear the thought of hearing the same old questions about her marital status again this Christmas, so she escaped.

What her mother and Isabella didn't know was, she hadn't chosen her career over a family. She just hadn't found a guy who made her head spin and stomach flutter, at least not for a while. Even so, while she was looking, she wouldn't apologize for making a good life for herself through her practice. She was helping people, made good money, had paid off her school loans, and was already building a nice nest egg. At this point in her life, why should she settle for anything other than love?

"In one mile, your destination is on your left," her GPS said.

Sophia kept her eyes on the road and did what came naturally. "Lord, calm my soul. And forgive me for lying to my mom. I just need a break in a quiet inn, far from all of the pressures and demands of my life. I know that you've already gone ahead of me and prepared exactly what my soul needs this Christmas. Thank you for that."

A light snow was falling, which meant there was a possibility of having a white Christmas. Given the elevation, she'd expected the ground to be covered in snow already from previous accumulations, but she only saw a patch here and there.

She hoped Mercy Inn was as quaint as Sarah Rose had described to her. Rose, a country music superstar who visited the inn a couple of years ago at Christmastime, came down with a bad cold during her recent tour stop in Atlanta. Her people had selected Sophia at random, hoping she could give Sarah something to help her throat hold out that evening.

The two of them hit it off right away. After chatting for a few minutes, Sarah recognized Sophia's need for a break from the pressures of her family and practice. And she knew just the place, run by an elderly couple who would go above and beyond to make it the best holiday experience she'd ever encountered.

"You might even find love there." Sarah winked at her from the examination table. "I did."

Sophia rolled her eyes, wrote Sarah a script, and darted to the computer after Sarah left the office to check out the Mercy Inn website. Everything about the place drew her in—the out-of-the-way location, the rustic cabins, the photo of the Christmas tree in the nook window. She clicked on the About page and read the place's history. The elderly couple had been running it for many decades. It seemed like it was ... well, just what the doctor ordered, so she'd booked the trip.

She pulled off Highway 17 and started down the gravel road toward the inn. Thirty seconds later, her breath caught in her throat as she saw the decorated Christmas tree in front of the lodge and another one through the window. And the snow-capped mountain peaks in the backdrop were stunning. The place was gorgeous. She couldn't wait to meet Ray and Alma.

* * *

Harold Taylor shook his head. How had he allowed Grace to talk him into this? It's not that he minded the impromptu trip to Colorado for Christmas. They needed to visit the state anyway. But why choose an inn where they would be around strangers?

3

Over the past couple of decades, he'd had his fill of people in Kansas City—many of whom were young, didn't respect the system, didn't have a strong work ethic, and were takers rather than givers. The entire country was sliding downhill as far as he was concerned.

"How much farther, honey?" Grace rummaged through her purse, looking for something.

Harold glanced up at the GPS on the windshield. "Twelve miles." Aspen and Alpine trees lined Highway 17. The only hint of civilization he'd seen over the last few miles was an antique shop. "Why'd you have to choose a place so far out in the boonies? I know you think I want to live like Ted Kaczynski, but this seems a bit much."

"Oh, it'll be fun." Grace finally pulled her cell phone out of her purse and powered it on. "Stop your fussing and just get us there. I don't like the fact that it's beginning to snow. Did you check the forecast this morning?"

"It didn't say anything about snow. We're close, so we don't have anything to worry about. What exactly will we be doing while we're at the inn? You said something about this being like a bed and breakfast. That sounds suspiciously like you're trying to get me to spend time around strangers."

Grace fiddled with her phone. "How did I find the weather forecast on this thing?"

When they'd first started dating at the age of fifteen in 1969, life was so much simpler—no computers, no cell phones, and no iPads. If you wanted to know the weather, you watched the ten o'clock news, or you tuned into KCMO on the AM dial in Kansas City.

"The app is called 'Weather,'" he said. "It's on the first screen you'll see after powering on the phone."

Grace swiped left, then right with her pointer finger, not seeming to hear him. "I don't see the blasted thing. Oh, wait. There it is." She tapped the app and gave it a few seconds. "Huh ... doesn't look like it's supposed to snow. But yet, look." She pointed to the flakes that were meandering from the sky.

Harold wished she'd just trust him. He'd told her he'd checked the forecast and no real accumulation was expected. Why did she always have to second guess him?

* * *

Ray Jordan checked the guest register at the front desk. He ran his fingers over the four visitors' names who would be arriving soon, stopping to pray for each one. As was usually the case, he didn't know their stories in advance, but that was part of the fun.

Alma Jordan was busy doing what she always did before the guests arrived—wiping down the tables in the breakfast nook and humming whatever Christmas tune was on the stereo. She stopped long enough to make eye contact with Ray. "I know I ask you this every year, but do we know anything specific about our visitors?" She continued wiping the tables, seeming to know the answer.

"Not a thing, other than their names."

"After the experiences we've had the last two years, with the roof caving in on our guests a couple of years ago and then a gunman showing up last year, I'm hoping for a much less stressful holiday season this time around."

"They have free will, as you know, and sometimes disasters

happen in a fallen world, so you never know what to expect. We just need to stay open to being led by the Spirit, no matter the circumstance."

Ray closed the registration book and joined Alma in the nook. "Let's pray for all of them, shall we?"

They grasped hands and bowed their heads.

Chapter 2

Trey Binford pulled his leased 2017 Ford Escape up to the Mercy Inn lodge and turned off the ignition. Was this a mistake? Just because his parents were off doing their own thing, separately, for the holidays didn't mean he needed to find such a remote place so far from Portland to make them think he had his own plans.

At the age of twenty-two, he didn't really care what his parents did now. They'd divorced three years ago and moved on, but it wasn't like they were around a lot when he was growing up anyway. He was pretty sure they'd both cheated on one another multiple times, which made for a tense upbringing, but whatever. What twenty-something didn't have a messy home life?

He could've stayed in his own apartment over the holiday, but when he'd seen Mercy Inn pop up in his social media feed one day, he checked out the website, and it looked perfect. He reminded himself of that as he sat there and considered bailing, but he'd traveled too far for that. He'd flown over a thousand miles from Portland to Sante Fe. And then rented a car and drove for another two-plus hours to Mercy Inn.

A woman with an almond-colored face and long dark hair stepped out of the car he'd parked next to, catching his eye. But she was too old for him—probably mid-thirties. He had high hopes for finding somebody to hang out with on this trip. It'd been too long. The problem was, nobody could measure up to his first love, Hannah.

The dark-haired woman was strike one.

He waited a couple of minutes before getting out and pulling his backpack from the trunk, still thinking this was a bad idea. By the time he entered the lodge, the woman who'd just walked in was helping herself to the snack table. He scanned the place, noticing six tables on a hardwood floor in a nook off to his right. The picture window that took up the entire wall in the nook was a nice touch.

"Hello, dear. My name is Alma. My husband, Ray, and I run the inn." She pointed in Ray's direction behind the counter. "He'll get you all checked in."

"Thank you."

After learning he'd be staying in a cabin named SIMON THE ZEALOT, named after the apostle, he nearly bolted.

"Relax, son," Ray said.

Trey's darting eyes must've given him away.

"We're here to make your stay this Christmas one to remember." Ray nodded in his wife's direction. "Help yourself to a sandwich or some snacks. You're in for a real treat. Alma is one of the best cooks you'll ever have the pleasure of meeting."

"Come on over, dear." Alma waved him toward a table that was full of food.

He shuffled in her direction. Should he offer her his hand?

She hugged him instead, then pulled away. "Help yourself to anything you see here."

He filled a plate and poured himself a cup of coffee. The woman who'd arrived shortly before he did was standing a few feet away, nibbling on a cookie.

"Trey, this is Dr. Gibbs," Alma said. "And Dr. Gibbs, this is Trey. Why don't the two of you get to know each other? I'll be back shortly."

"Call me Sophia." She extended her hand.

He shook it. "I'm Trey. Nice to meet you."

"Nice to meet you too. Looks like we're the first arrivals for the holidays, huh? Shall we?" She pulled out one of the chairs at the closest table and sat down.

Trey followed her lead. "I wonder how many guests they are expecting." He took a bite of his roast beef sandwich. "I'm already having second thoughts about coming."

Sophia took a sip of her coffee. "Oh, this really hits the spot." She took another drink. "What makes you skeptical?"

Here we go. Another older person who wants to judge me three seconds after we met. "I like to think of it as being real, but your generation and the ones after it all seem to think all Millennials are skeptics. That's cool. Maybe we are, but we have good reason to be."

"You misunderstood." Sophia held up her hands. "I was just referring to your comment about having second thoughts about being here."

"Oh, sorry. I'm a little defensive about the way older people see me sometimes."

"Ouch. Now I'm the one who should be offended." But her smile told him she was just kidding around.

Even so, he hoped more guests who were closer to his age would be showing up soon.

* * *

"So, do you want to tell me what's really going on with this trip?" Harold asked. "Why all the secrecy about this inn? Why not just get a regular hotel room somewhere in southern Colorado for a week so we can explore the area with a realtor? You aren't trying to sneak me into some Amway presentation, are you?"

She couldn't help but laugh at Harold's dry sense of humor. In reality, she wasn't being secretive. She had a feeling about the place the first time she saw an ad for it while shopping online one day. She clicked the link to the Mercy Inn website on a whim and she was drawn to the place. Something about the inn's owners, Ray and Alma, and their down-home style of waiting on guests, made her want to experience Christmas with them.

For years, she'd been the one who was responsible for cooking Christmas dinner for the extended family, buying all the gifts, and making sure everybody was taken care of. After the kids got older and moved out, and Harold became more reclusive, her responsibilities lightened somewhat, but still, she wanted someone to take care of her during the holidays for once.

But something deeper was going on—something she couldn't put her finger on when it came to what really drew her to Mercy Inn. Maybe it was the name of the place. She knew Harold wouldn't be crazy about the idea of spending the holiday with other people, but she needed help with him. He was growing angrier with each passing year as the culture slid downhill in his opinion.

Maybe it was, but couldn't they just live out their retirement years in peace and leave the political reform to the next generation? Why did he care so much?

"I've already told you that I want somebody to pamper us during the holidays," she said. "I think I deserve a break. I want to enjoy the magic of the season. I want something different than cooking a meal, opening gifts, and then cleaning the house for the next two hours."

Harold didn't say anything for a few seconds. "I think you've been watching too much TV. The magic of Christmas—it's all make-believe, created by greeting card companies to exploit your sentimentalism. It's a sham. And who knows what sort of causes they are supporting?"

In recent years, Grace was finding it more difficult to talk about the most seemingly innocuous of topics with him. He was quick to chastise her for nearly everything. According to Harold, the gas station she'd been patronizing for years was now selling terrorist-sponsored gasoline. The dollar store she frequented was full of goods and services manufactured by communists for the sole purpose of weakening American commerce. On and on it went. She was tired of it all, but anytime she protested, Harold would shake his head and claim she'd been duped, like "all the rest of them," whoever they might be.

"Just humor me for this one holiday," Grace said. "By this time next year, we'll be settled into our new place here in Colorado."

"I like the sound of that."

* * *

Harold opened the door to the inn, allowing Grace to enter in front of him. He still believed in opening doors for women, no matter what modern culture might think. She might have tricked him into coming here, but he could still show that he was a gentleman.

After registering at the front desk, and learning they were staying in a cabin named ANDREW, a woman named Alma introduced them to two other guests—a doctor named Sophia and a hipster named Trey.

Sophia smiled and shook Grace's hand, then his. She was nice enough, but she was a doctor and he didn't trust doctors. And one glance at Trey told him everything he needed to know. The kid was wearing ratty jeans that sagged off his hips and a black hoodie with his sleeves pushed up, exposing a tattoo of some bizarre-looking symbol on his forearm. And he oozed attitude, like most people his age.

Grace took a seat at Trey and Sophia's table, always the social butterfly. He would've preferred a table to themselves—or better yet, checking into their room. Alma brought them both a steaming mug of coffee and a few cookies on a plate. One sip nearly dropped him to his knees. It was the sweetest drink he'd ever tasted.

"Yowza! What in the world is in this stuff? Is it one hundred percent sugar? What ever happened to black coffee?"

"Oh, dear. I'm sorry, Mr. Taylor. It's a drink called 'Christmas Delight.' Most of our guests love it. But you're right, it's quite sweet. Let me brew you some black coffee. I'll be right back."

She was gone before he could stop her. Who drinks coffee in the late afternoon anyway? The whole country had gone mad about coffee. They were lemmings. But what was a guy to do? When in southern Colorado, do as southern Coloradoans do.

Ray approached them. "Now that everybody is here, Alma and I want to welcome you to Mercy Inn. We trust you will find your accommodations to your liking. You won't have to worry about a thing while you're here. As you probably saw on the website, we supply all the food and entertainment—all in the hopes that you'll have a Christmas to remember."

"Wait, this is it? Nobody else is coming?"

Apparently, the hipster was hoping to find a lady friend while he was here. Unless the doctor was willing to rob the cradle, he was going to be out of luck.

"This is it, Mr. Binford." Ray waved his hands around the room. "It'll make for an intimate setting for the holidays, won't it?"

"What exactly will we be doing? Can I hang out in my room the whole time?"

"You can do anything you want, Mr. Binford. But Alma and I hope you'll join us for the festivities. We'll play games, probably hum along to a Christmas carol or two, feast, and get to know one another better."

"How lame."

"Hey, you signed up for this buddy," Harold said. "Give it a chance." He had to admit though, the kid had a point.

The hipster shot to his feet. "You got a problem with me, old man?"

If he decked Trey, it might put a damper on the old Christmas spirit. But that didn't mean he didn't want to. He balled both fists a couple of times, trying to think of something clever to say. But nothing came, so he issued a warning instead. "Watch yourself, buddy."

Ray stepped between them and put his arms out. "Gentlemen, please. Settle down. We'll have none of that here. This would be a good time for everyone to check out their rooms and to let us know if you need anything. We'll meet back here in thirty minutes."

What had Grace gotten them into? This was the exact reason

Harold wanted to move away from Kansas City and out onto their own acreage—so he wouldn't have to deal with vermin like this. And now he was going to have to spend the next two and a half days with this guy?

Chapter 3

G race finished putting their clothes away and took a seat on the bed. "Honey, what was that all about back there?"

Harold glanced up from the couch, where he was watching some political television show in which everybody was screaming at each other. How he could watch such a thing was beyond her.

"The kid is a punk." Harold waved the remote control.

She smoothed the bedspread. "His name is Trey, and let's give him a chance. Even if he has a bit of an attitude, we don't know his story. Maybe you could cut him a little slack since it's Christmas."

Harold hit the mute button. "How would knowing his story matter?"

Grace couldn't look him in the eye, but she'd needed to confront him about his growing cynicism for some time now. "What happened to you, Harold? You never used to be so bitter and angry."

She knew the answer. It was simply a difference in opinion between generations. Harold's generation—Baby Boomers—believed in working hard, taking responsibility, and climbing the latter—at least some of them did. Of course, they hadn't always been that way. They, too, had been young once—embracing the sexual revolution, as it was called. They shucked off the rigidity of their parents' generation in favor of freedom, but it had come with a price.

A few of their friends died as a result of poor lifestyle choices. Too many marriages fell apart due to high levels of infidelity. And their children grew up in broken homes with messy lives, blaming their parents when things went wrong. But by the time Boomers were in charge, they'd mellowed. They still had their individualistic spirit, but they used it to advance businesses, careers, and social status.

They tended to forget they were young once too. And now, ironically, two generations later, Millennials didn't seem to trust the Boomers or their way of life. Millennials had their own ideas about the way things ought to be, and they weren't interested in listening to Boomers. Boomers saw that as disrespect. And Harold seemed to be at the front of the line when it came to such feelings.

Now they were going to be spending Christmas with Trey, and Grace wasn't sure how that could possibly work. She considered calling around to see if she could find another hotel or inn nearby. She could have a nice quiet Christmas with Harold somewhere else and hit the ground running the day after Christmas in search of a place to live.

Harold sat up on the couch. "You know what happened to me, Grace. It's the same thing that happened to you. Our way of life, our way of thinking, everything we've worked for is being torn down by young thugs who care more about where their next fix is coming from than they do about being productive members of society. And I can't stand that." He tossed the remote onto the coffee table.

"Isn't it possible to fight the war while still giving individuals the benefit of the doubt?" She finally made eye contact with him. "And even if they are immature, they can still come around, but not if we don't have conversations with them—not if they don't see why we believe what we believe."

Harold shook his head.

"But if you want, I'll see if I can find us another place to stay for the holidays. There has to be another inn nearby."

"It might be a good idea, at least as a backup plan. I think I'd enjoy the holiday more if it were just you and me."

Grace called information. Harold had his laptop she could've used, but she wasn't familiar with it. The only computer she could find her way around was the old desktop they had at home. And it was on its last legs. A couple of minutes after placing the call, she had three options within thirty miles—all of which had vacancies.

"Okay, so we have options," she said. "What do you say we go back up to the lodge and give it one last try. If you still want to leave, we'll pack our bags and stay the night in one of these other places."

"Deal."

* * *

This wasn't what Sophia had signed up for. The Mercy Inn website promised a Christmas oasis, but so far, it was anything but. She finished unpacking, taking note of the fireplace in the corner. Maybe she'd get a fire going when she returned to her room later. She was expecting a small-town homey environment. Instead, she appeared to have walked into the middle of a culture war—one she didn't understand or care to try to figure out. She had enough of her own problems.

Her cell phone chirped. Maybe it was Anthony. They'd only been on a couple of dates, but she was drawn to him—enough to be checking her phone more often than a grown woman ought to. It turned out to be her mother who wanted to apologize.

"All is forgiven," Sophia typed in response. "I just needed to get away to clear my head." She hit send.

She hadn't told her mother about Anthony yet because he wasn't the kind of guy she'd approve of. He made a meager income as an artistic painter and her mother would never understand a relationship—if it ever came to that—in which Sophia made more money than her boyfriend.

She scrolled back through her messages and found Anthony's name. Maybe she'd missed a text from him. Nope. He hadn't sent anything in nearly a week. Clearly, he wasn't interested, which was fine. She hadn't invested any emotions in him yet. But not having a love interest during the holidays was going to be rough. She'd never needed a man, but that didn't mean she didn't want one.

Light snow outside her window caught her attention. She walked over and enjoyed the scene for a few seconds. She rarely got to see snow in Atlanta. While she didn't want to get stuck here, she was still hoping for an inch or two to make things a bit more festive. She raised her cell phone and snapped a photo through the window.

After taking a seat on the couch, she posted the photo on social media with this caption: "Looks like I'm in for a white Christmas this year! Don't be jealous, Atlanta." She watched as the "likes" and comments began rolling in.

"No fair!" wrote one of the nurses from her office.

"You can keep the snow," wrote a friend from high school.

"Looks like heaven!" wrote her hairdresser.

If they only knew what I walked into here. She glanced at her watch. It was time to head back to the inn for whatever Alma had planned for the evening. Hopefully, things would be calmer between Harold and Trey. Harold certainly had an ax to grind, but it was Christmas. Surely, they could all find a way to get into the Christmas spirit.

She bundled up and headed back to the lodge. Ray was waiting and held the door open for her.

"Come on in, Sophia." He swung the door open wide. "Grab a sandwich and something to drink, then take a seat by the fireplace in the living room. Alma wants all of us to get to know each other a little better."

She thanked him, poured another cup of coffee, made a sandwich, and took a seat on the couch, directly across from the fireplace. Trey was already there, seated in a rocking chair, which surprised her. She thought he might leave before this thing even got started.

He nodded in her direction. "Sophia."

"Trey."

Awkward silence.

This idea of spending Christmas with total strangers sounded better in theory than in practice. "So, where are you from, and what made you decide to make this trip?"

He took a sip of his coffee, as if he were contemplating how much he wanted to reveal. "I live in Portland, and I wanted a change of scenery this Christmas. How about you?"

That was pretty vague, but maybe if she opened up a bit to him, he'd let his guard down. "I'm from Atlanta, and I'm sort

19

of running away from my family for the holidays. They are relentless when it comes to my marital status—they think I should be settled down by now." She used air quotes around the words "settled down" and rolled her eyes to turn it into a joke.

"Doesn't seem like it should be any of their business. Why would they care?" Trey rocked back and forth, seeming to get more comfortable.

His take was a breath of fresh air. "My mom—I love her. I really do. But I think she's embarrassed when she meets with her friends since she doesn't have an announcement to make about me." She used air quotes again around the word "announcement."

"That's not really fair to you. You have your own life to live."

"I wish she saw it that way."

* * *

Trey admired Sophia's honesty. He wasn't sure he was ready to let her into his own world though.

Alma joined them, taking a seat in the rocking chair opposite Trey. "Well, are you two getting to know each other a little better?"

"We are," Sophia said. "This is such a great facility. How long have you and Ray been running it?"

"Oh, you wouldn't believe it if I told him, dear." Alma wiggled her eyebrows. "Let's just say we've been at this for longer than you've been alive." She glanced at her watch. "I wonder where the Taylors are? They should've been here by now."

"Do you ever get any unannounced drop-in guests during the

holidays?" Sophia asked.

"Can't say that we do, dear. So many people have plans with family or friends during the holidays. Our guests usually have a reason to avoid such gatherings, at least for that particular year."

Everyone sat in silence for a few seconds, listening to the roar of the fire Ray had built while an ancient version of "Jingle Bells" played on the stereo.

The Taylors entered the lodge and headed for the living room. Alma invited them to make a plate of food, but they both said they were full from snacking on the road, so she asked them to take a seat.

Harold pointed for Grace to sit next to Sophia on the couch while he sat on the end, the farthest seat from Trey. Trey was happy about that. Why even pretend to respect each other? He still couldn't believe he was stuck here with a bunch of old people. Sophia seemed cool, but even she was nearly old enough to be his mother.

The room buzzed to life with chitchat. Ray joined them and threw another log on the fire before taking a seat in a rocking chair next to Alma.

Ray fidgeted with a stack of index cards. "Welcome everybody. This first night we like to get to know one another by playing a game we call 'Nicebreaker.'"

Trey wasn't the only one to groan. Harold voiced his displeasure just as loudly. This was going to be the lamest Christmas ever.

"Don't knock it until you've tried it." Ray shuffled the cards. "But if you decide you don't like it, we won't play any more rounds this weekend. I'm sure Alma has lots of other things we could do instead."

Everybody looked toward her for an answer. Her smirk told them she probably wasn't going to let them in on her secret. "I certainly have other fun activities planned for us, and a few on standby, just in case. But nobody has to do anything they don't want to. This is supposed to be fun—maybe a throwback to the types of Christmases you had as a kid."

"Does this mean we get gifts?" Trey knew better, but he had to ask.

"It does, in fact." Alma pointed toward the tree in the corner. "They've already been wrapped."

As nice as it was, how could she have purchased gifts for them without even knowing them?

Chapter 4

Games and gifts? Harold supposed it wouldn't be the end of the world. He would've preferred a gentlemanly game of Gin Rummy, but Nicebreaker would have to do. If this turned out to be a disaster, they could leave. *And we better not get charged here for the night.*

Ray cleared his throat and began to shuffle the cards. "The game is pretty simple. There really aren't any rules, per se. I'll pass these cards around. Take five of them. But keep them face down so you cannot see the questions. Once everybody has his or her cards, we'll take turns asking each other the questions on the cards. You don't have to ask people in any certain order, but you can only ask each person one question."

"Don't forget, dear, they have to name the person they want to ask the question *before* they flip the card."

Ray nodded. "I always forget to mention that."

"That way, nobody can get upset with the questioner," Alma said. "But if you get a question that makes you feel uncomfortable or you don't want to answer, you don't have to. This is supposed to be fun, while also helping us to learn a little about you."

"By the end of the night, we'll all be singing Kumbaya, right?" Harold asked.

"Harold, do you have to be so negative?" Grace shook her head.

"If the situation warrants it."

"Carry on with the instructions," Grace said. "Sorry for the interruption.

Harold hated it when Grace apologized for him, but he knew better than to pick a fight with her in front of everybody. He'd never hear the end of it. But he stored her infraction away in his memory for safekeeping.

Something rubbed one of his legs. Before he could look down, whatever it was, jumped into his lap.

"Whoa."

Grace giggled.

"That's Snowball, our lodge cat," Alma said. "We named him that for obvious reasons. Generally, he chooses one guest each year to snuggle up with, and it looks like he's already made his decision. I hope you don't mind, dear."

"I'm usually of the opinion that animals belong outside." Harold raised his arms, not wanting to get scratched.

Snowball pranced in circles in his lap, apparently in search of the perfect place to plop down. Finally, he found it. He curled up in a ball, placing one of his back paws against Harold's stomach. Harold had to admit, Snowball was adorable. He lowered his arms and began to rub Snowball's belly, making Snowball a friend for life. His purr nearly drowned out the music. Apparently, this little guy was content.

"By the way, the reason some of these cards are a little worse for wear is that they've been in circulation for many years." Ray shuffled them one more time. "Every year, our guests get to write their own question on a card and it gets added to the stack."

"Oh, I can't wait to do that," Grace said.

Ray glanced at Alma, making Harold suspicious. Ray wasn't telling them something. By why keep information about a stupid game to himself?

"This sounds like fun," Sophia said. "Who goes first?"

Ray began to pass the cards around. "Let's start with Harold."

"Before we get started, does anybody want a refill on your coffee?" Alma stood, ready to serve. "Or maybe a cookie or two?"

Trey stood. "I think I'll take a refill. You've got some black coffee over there, right? As good as the Christmas Delight tastes, it's too sweet for me."

"Sure thing, dear. Let me have your mug." She started for the nook. "Anybody else?"

Everybody else was good.

This all had a 1950s feel to it—with the Christmas music in the background, the game they were about to play, and everybody gathered in front of a fireplace with a mountain of presents to be opened. And remarkably, most people weren't checking their cell phones every three seconds. The only guilty party so far was Sophia, and she was a doctor, so maybe she had a good reason.

What was the story with the kid though? Why wasn't Trey checking his social media accounts? Maybe Trey was a vagabond and didn't have the money for a phone. That would certainly explain it. But if that were the case, how could he have afforded this little vacation? *His parents probably provided it for him.*

Alma returned with Trey's coffee and Ray nodded at Harold for him to begin. "Who is your first choice, Harold?"

Let's go with the safe choice. "Grace." He pulled a card out of the middle of his stack and flipped it over. "Describe your first cell phone. And how long did it take you to learn how to use it?"

Oh, brother. The entire world is obsessed with cell phones.

* * *

Instinctively, Grace reached inside her purse and pulled out her current phone. "My first cell phone was the original iPhone. Our daughter, Gail, got it for me for Christmas in 2007, I think. I had no idea how to use the blasted thing, but she spent the holidays with us that year and taught me how to do the basics before she went back home."

"That was before social media, wasn't it?" Sophia asked. "What did you use it for?"

"Texting and Facetime, mostly. I loved being able to chat with our grandchildren face to face." She caught Harold rolling his eyes. "What?"

"Gail and her family life in Texas," Harold said. "We live in Kansas City. Talking to them on a video stream over an iPhone is hardly the same as face to face."

"Oh, you know what I meant."

Grace couldn't help but be saddened by the man Harold had become. Nobody would believe it now, but when they first met, way back in high school, he was a fun-loving guy. He took her to school dances, cracked jokes, and he became her rock as the years progressed—especially after she'd contracted an unknown virus in her early thirties that almost took her life. Thankfully, it left her body as mysteriously as it had entered it. But before that, Harold had kept the mood light as he took her to visit one doctor after another. He did all the housework. Cooked often. And was as close to being a model husband as they come.

Everything seemed to change on September 11, 2001, when the country was attacked. Never one to follow politics before that date, he began to consume political shows on television and radio. And he was always quick to share what he was learning with her.

As an apolitical person, she listened as best she could, all the while growing more concerned by the day at the changes she saw in Harold. He went from jovial to jaded over the course of a few weeks. And he developed a disdain for younger generations. Now he seemed to distrust nearly everything and everybody. Technology was no exception.

"You know that the NSA is tracking you on that thing, right?" Harold asked.

Grace rolled her eyes. This was exactly what she'd been trying to avoid when she booked this trip. She wanted an old-fashioned Christmas without all of the drama and tension, but clearly, that wasn't going to happen—not here, especially if Trey, or even Sophia, answered a question in a way Harold didn't appreciate. They wouldn't be staying the night here. She was sure of it. Her anger toward Harold began to boil below the surface.

"It's your turn, dear." Alma sat back in her rocking chair.

There was no way in the world Grace was going to pick Trey. "I choose Sophia." She flipped a card from her stack. "Who is the first person who comes to mind whenever you hear a love song?"

This could be an interesting answer. Sophia wasn't wearing a ring, but surely she had at least one great love in her past. Maybe her answer would calm the tension in the room.

27

* * *

"I guess that question presupposes that all of us have just one such love over the course of our lifetime, or, at the very least, that one stands out more than any other." Sophia was buying time. But she suspected that nobody really needed to think about the answer to this question.

On her trip from Atlanta, she was flipping through the radio dial somewhere across Kansas when she came across a station playing '90s music. Her breath caught in her throat when she heard the opening notes of "More Than Words" by Extreme—a song about showing the person you love that you really do love him or her without necessarily needing to say the words.

In every way possible, it was the anthem for her first love. The song had been out for five or six years by the time they had started dating, but you could still hear it on the radio every once in a while. And it became their song.

"Sounds like someone doesn't really want to answer the question," Harold said.

"No pressure, dear."

"His name is Greg. We met in college." She used a measured tone. "We dated for two years but split up because we wanted different things. He's the one I still think about whenever I hear a love song all these years later."

"Have you searched for him online?" Trey asked.

She sighed. She'd sound like a stalker if she admitted it, but seriously, who hadn't looked up an ex online? "I don't spend a lot of time living in the past."

"That really didn't answer my question, but it's cool if you don't want to."

He held his chin high, and her face turned warm. It was like he was taking the high ground on an issue that wasn't high-ground material. She really wanted to cut this kid some slack, but he was making it difficult.

"I've looked him up. He got everything he ever wanted—the perfect career, lots of friends, and I'm sure he has a family."

"His social media accounts don't specify?" Trey said.

"They don't, but we aren't 'friends' there. I didn't want to open that can of worms."

"Maybe he's the one," Trey said.

His words made her heart hurt. She'd often wondered about what might've been. Had she made the wrong decision to walk away from the relationship all those years ago? She doubted it. He didn't fight for the relationship any harder than she did. And they really did want different things.

"This is probably more than I should admit, but I'll say this—we had chemistry. We didn't have to express our affection for one another in words, as the song expressed. We could simply exist in the same space, knowing we'd rather be there than any other place on earth."

"I'll Be Home on Christmas Day" by Elvis played on the stereo in the background, making her feel even more nostalgic. Her grandfather was an Elvis fan.

"Sounds like you've got it bad, girl." Trey stroked his chin. "You ought to hit him up. See where it goes. If he's married, or with somebody, so be it. Move on. But if he isn't, then—"

"Enough about my love life." Sophia reached for the index cards, anxious to put Trey in the hot seat. "I choose Trey."

He rolled his eyes.

She pulled a card from the bottom of her pile and flipped it. "If you could be anywhere else but here, where would you be, and why?"

* * *

Maybe if he told them his story, he'd earn a little respect. "We're all running from something, right? I'm no different."

"Speak for yourself, buddy," Harold said.

"I'm guessing that people like me make you nervous because you can't cope with people who don't think like you do."

Harold glared at him. Apparently, he wasn't used to people speaking the truth to him. Trey was only happy to do so.

"I chose this place because I wanted to be anywhere but Portland. My parents split when I was young. It was cool. Most of my friends grew up in similar situations. I lived with my dad because my mom—well, let's just say she had her problems."

Snowball woke up, jumped out of Harold's lap, and approached Trey. Trey patted his lap and Snowball was happy to oblige, springing into his lap and plopping down.

Trey stroked his fur from head to tail. "But my old man had his issues too. He drank. A lot. When I turned eighteen, he gave me twenty-four hours to find a place of my own. I was working a bit here and there but didn't have enough money to move out. I couch-hopped for a while, until my friends got tired of it, and then ended up on the streets."

"That's horrible, dear."

"I got along okay. One night, I went to a homeless shelter and found out about an apprentice program for graphic artists. I'd always been interested in that and had taken some classes in high school, so I asked them to hook me up. It didn't pay much, but enough to get a run-down studio apartment in the ghetto."

"How long did it take to complete the internship?" Sophia took a sip of her coffee.

"A full school year. The company hired me full-time after that. It put me on my feet financially, but holidays were so difficult. My parents were still a mess. We still don't talk much these days." He paused for a few seconds. "I couldn't take sitting in that apartment by myself again over Christmas."

Trey was hesitant to lift his eyes to read the room, but he took a chance. Grace's eyes glistened. So did Alma's. And Sophia pursed her lips in sympathy. Harold was a statue though. It didn't surprise or even offend Trey. Harold reminded Trey of his old man—detached, unfeeling, uncaring.

"So, the answer to Sophia's question is, I sought out this place because I wanted to be around people this Christmas. And honestly, I was hoping to find a girl. If I could be anywhere but here, I guess it would be spending time with a woman who loves me. I had that once. I hope to find it again."

"We're glad you're here, dear."

Harold's eyes told him otherwise. But everyone else was listening to his story and showing interest in him. That felt pretty good.

"Enough about me," Trey said. "It's my turn to ask a question, right?"

Chapter 5

Trey had just described everything that was wrong with America. One broken generation leads to the next. Harold felt for the kid as he listened to his story, but at some point, Trey needed to get a clue and make a better life for himself. Securing an internship was a good start, but he seemed incapable of making human connections. That didn't surprise Harold, given his cocky attitude.

"This question is for Harold." Trey flipped an index card. "When you come to the end of your life, what do you think you'll be most proud of, and why?"

"I'll be proud of a lot of things, I imagine—that I married up, had two children I'm proud of, served my country, worked hard my whole life as a machinist, and fought for what I believed in."

"Care to go into more detail about one of those?" Ray said. "Imagine you're lying on your deathbed. Which one will you be thinking about most?"

"I'm proud of my family, of course. They are all upstanding people who love one another—just the way a family should. But I feel like they are more of a blessing—something that has been given to me, rather than something I should be proud of accomplishing."

Ray nodded.

"What I'm most proud of is connected to my family though. On my deathbed, I'll be thinking about the way I stood for truth during a time period in which people no longer accept such a notion. I'll be proud of being part of the last generation who'll remember this country when she was at her best."

"Are you referring to the 1950s when segregation reigned and women were barefoot and pregnant?" Trey asked. "Or maybe to the 1980s when greed was celebrated?"

Harold's face turned hot. "I'll be most proud of standing against people like you." He pointed at Trey.

"You have an over-idealized view," Trey said. "This country has always been about oppression. We took the land from Native Americans and forced them onto reservations. We bought slaves to work the land. African Americans were only considered three-fifths of a person. Even now, non-whites can't drive down the street without the fear of being profiled by the police. If you're proud of that heritage, then you're misguided."

Harold's blood pressure was rising by the second. He needed to calm down. If he let this punk rile him up in front of everybody, Trey would appear to have won the argument. He could outreason Trey any day.

"Has our country made mistakes?" Harold asked. "Of course. Many. That's what happens in a free society. But we always figure it out. We always turn things around. We always end up offering more freedom, not less. More opportunity, not less. Women have more rights now than ever. The country elected an African American president in 2008. And I'm hopeful that racial profiling will eventually be a thing of the past. Can't you at least see the progress we've made?"

"What I see is the old guard resisting change and opportunity for those who don't look like they do." Trey's words were measured, calculated even. He was good. Better than Harold had given him credit for. "This progression that you're talking about is happening despite, not because of, the people who claim America's heritage is so great."

Harold tapped his foot, doing everything he could to avoid lashing out in anger. "Our forefathers were too busy making sacrifices for the sake of freedom to get everything exactly right. They picked up arms to form and protect our fledgling nation. And many lived through extremely difficult financial times. You have no idea what they went through."

"Did you miss the part of my story in which I told you I was homeless? What I didn't tell you was how hungry I was, and how I had to go dumpster diving at McDonald's. Or how cold I got on nights when the homeless shelter was full and I had to curl up on a park bench using a newspaper as a blanket. Don't tell me that I don't understand hardship, old man."

"Enough with the name-calling," Ray said. "Let's move on with the game. This is supposed to help bring us together, not tear us apart."

* * *

Alma stepped in to try to move the game along. She chose Grace and flipped a card. "What is your favorite photo, and why?"

Alma had her eye on Grace. Despite all the saber-rattling going on between Harold and Trey, Alma was concerned that Grace might get lost in all the noise. She seemed timid—almost like she was hiding something, and Alma was hoping to get to the bottom of it before everybody left in three days.

Grace reached for her phone, apparently searching for the photo. She found it rather quickly, but then set the phone down in her lap. "Before Harold and I got married, we dated for six years—mostly during high school, and then a couple of years afterward. We attended school dances often, and we had the time of our lives." She paused for a moment, as if she were caught up in one of those memories.

"Our junior year, we attended a dance shortly before Christmas break. Do you remember that dance, honey?" Grace put her hand on Harold's knee.

He nodded. "How could I forget?"

Alma liked where this was headed. Grace was trying to pull him back to a simpler time to remind him of who he was before he became so bitter.

"Anyway, we were on the dance floor most of the night. We broke out in a sweat to 'Smoke on the Water,' 'Live and Let Die,' 'You're So Vain,' and 'Bad, Bad Leroy Brown.'"

"And then the DJ played 'My Love' by Wings," Harold said.

"I never felt more alive than when you held me close during that slow dance." Grace closed her eyes. "I was sort of hoping for an eight-minute dance-floor mix, but I didn't get my wish." Her smile held a hint of sadness. "But after the song, Harold grabbed my hand, led me off the dance floor, and took me to a back corner where a photographer was set up. Harold plunked down a few dollars and asked me to choose a background. I went with a park scene with a pond in the distance."

She turned her phone around to show everyone the photo of two teenagers who were smiling and lost in love.

It warmed Alma's heart. "Oh, what a beautiful memory. Why is this particular photo your favorite?"

"We don't have many photos of us from our high school years.

Just a few, in fact. But this one captures us so well, I think."

"What a beautiful story, Grace." Sophia's voice cracked. "That's exactly how it's supposed to be. We find somebody when we're young, get married, and spend the rest of our lives together."

Grace reached over and rubbed Sophia's shoulder. "It's the way things were done back then. Your generation has it so much harder now. Seems like nobody wants to marry until much later."

Alma was pleased to see the bond forming between Grace and Sophia. She had a feeling that the two would remain in touch. They needed each other.

* * *

Ray asked Alma the final question of the first round. One he'd heard her answer several times about her most embarrassing hairstyle. But Alma acted like it was the first time she'd ever received the question, explaining that she used to sport a beehive hairdo.

"I did too!" Grace said.

"What's a beehive hairdo?" Trey said.

"We'd grow our hair long, dear, and then wrap it around and around on top of our head."

"I feel like you're describing an ice cream cone," Trey said.

"That's not far from the truth." Grace laughed.

Despite the laugh and the connection that seemed to be forming between Grace and Sophia, Ray was concerned. In all the years they'd been using this game to get to the heart of what their guests cared about and feared, he'd never seen it reveal such differences in people like it had between Harold and Trey. He sensed it was time to wrap things up for the evening with a promise of good things to come.

Ray turned off the stereo. "All right, everybody. Let's get a good night's sleep. Alma has a fun day of activities planned for everybody tomorrow. In fact," he pointed at the Christmas tree, "we'll dig into those tomorrow morning, first thing after breakfast."

"But tomorrow is only Christmas Eve," Grace said. "Shouldn't we wait until Christmas morning?"

"We have even more planned for you for Christmas Day."

"More, as in more gifts?" Trey said.

"A different sort of gift," Ray said. "That's all I can say right now. I'm sworn to secrecy." He pretended to zip his lips. In reality, he didn't even know himself, but as he was talking, he was given instructions from on high.

After everybody left the lodge and headed for their rooms, Ray felt impressed to fetch specific Christmas albums out of their personal collection and have them ready to play at a moment's notice.

Albums? I'm not even sure if the record player still functions properly. We stopped using albums at the inn in the late 1970s. In fact, he was fairly certain that the last time they used the old record player, the needle malfunctioned and needed to be replaced. He never got around to it because 8-track players were taking off at the time. But who was he to argue?

He left Alma to her tasks and headed for their living quarters. He remembered storing the record player and a modest set of speakers at the bottom of their living room closet, and since then, it had probably been buried under piles of clothes and artifacts from Christmases past. When he pulled the closet door open, sure enough, the record player was right where he remembered it.

It took him a few minutes to move everything that was on top of it and to hoist it and the speakers onto the couch. He wiped the dust off the cover with his hands and gently eased it open to check the needle. He ran his forefinger where the needle was supposed to be located and it nearly cut him.

"What in the world?"

The record player had a brand new needle already inserted into its arm. Alma couldn't have done such a thing. Sure, she was an angel, but she left technology to him. This was a heavenly action. Something big was about to take place. He could feel it.

Now, he needed to find a list of albums—some of which he wasn't even sure he owned. But he had a feeling they would be there, no matter whether he owned them or not. And since he used to file his albums in alphabetical order by artist, he should have the albums pulled out and ready to go in no time.

He dug deeper inside the closet in search of a box labeled "Christmas albums." Five minutes later, he'd found every album he was looking for. And shortly after that, he had the record player and speakers set up above the fireplace in the lodge's common living room. As he was finishing up, he received a directive to hide the albums for now. Before he could do so, Alma approached him.

"So, what gives, dear? What do you have planned for Christmas Day?"

"All I know so far is, it involves our old record player and a pile of albums I was told to have ready."

"What do you think it could mean?" Alma picked up the dirty coffee mugs and empty plates.

Ray joined her. "Obviously, music means something to all our guests in some form or fashion. Let's just see what happens."

They finished cleaning and plopped down on the couch. A nagging question continued to run through Ray's mind, so he voiced it to Alma. "How far do we let things escalate between Harold and Trey?" Conflict wasn't necessarily a bad thing because it could cause introspection, and introspection could lead to change. But if it got too far out of hand, they could end up going after each other.

"It's uncomfortable to watch, no doubt," Alma said. "But it seems like it's necessary. Neither one is going to get what he came for if he doesn't face his own flaws, limitations, and perspectives."

Ray nodded. "But before that can happen, Harold and Grace have to stick around. His argument with Trey tonight might cause them to find a new place to stay. I wouldn't be at all surprised to wake up tomorrow and find out that they left."

"They are free to make that choice, as you know, dear. It isn't our responsibility to force anything. We're just here to facilitate change. It's up to them after that."

Chapter 6

Sophia tossed and turned after climbing into her bed. After being asked about Greg, and then hearing Harold and Grace's love story, it was hard not to think that maybe Greg was the one who got away. Why had he kept his marital status such a secret on social media? She'd found a Florida address and phone number for him online, but she was terrified to call it. What if his wife answered?

She hadn't really lied to the group earlier when she said they split because they wanted different things. Greg wanted another girl—a classmate who was prettier than Sophia, at least in Sophia's mind.

Sophia had never had any problems attracting men, all of whom told her she was beautiful, but she knew there was a difference between being attractive and being a stunner, and she was no stunner. Maybe Greg was bald with a beer belly by now. It would serve him right. Not that she'd care though. She was drawn to the way he made her feel about herself—at least until he left her for someone else.

Sophia glanced at the clock on the nightstand. It was nearly three o'clock in the morning. At this rate, she felt like she'd never get to sleep. Her mind was racing with too many questions, too many unknowns. If the first day at Mercy Inn was any indication, these next two days were going to be an emotional roller coaster—one that might keep leading back to Greg. But what about Anthony? Shouldn't she give him a chance? *He'd have to care enough to stay in contact with me.*

Her cell phone chirped. It was a nurse. She was texting Sophia to let her know that one of her patients, a forty-seven-year-old male named Jonathan Jefferies, had a massive heart attack and it didn't look good for him. Sophia said a short prayer for him and hoped he had all his affairs in order. She suspected that he did. He was a well-known businessman in Atlanta and presumably had many assets.

Life is so short. Mr. Jefferies was just nine years older than she was, and his life might already be drawing to a close. Now was not the time to wait for something to happen. She responded to the nurse with a quick thank you, asking her to keep Sophia in the loop. She needed her iPad. She rolled out of bed to get it and stubbed her big toe on the nightstand. She grabbed her foot, pulling it upward to examine the damage, but it was no use. It was too dark. Eventually, she found the light switch and flipped it on.

She took a seat in a chair by the door and examined her toe. She couldn't see any blood, and it didn't appear to be broken, but it was tender. She limped over to the dresser, grabbed her iPad, flipped the light off, and plopped back into bed—angry at herself for being such a klutz.

As she tried to put her throbbing toe out of her mind, she decided to do a little comparison game. She had never spent much time looking for information about Anthony, which, she realized at that moment, probably said a lot about how she felt about him. That could change, once she got to know him, but now that she'd been thinking about Greg, she preferred the history she had with him.

She started with Anthony, finding him on social media. His life really wasn't an open book. He posted mostly about sports—he was a diehard Atlanta Falcons and Atlanta Braves fan, and he posted a lot about how good the SEC was, whatever that meant. He also posted a few Bible verses. She found one from last Christmas: "For unto you is born this day in the city of David a Savior, who is Christ the Lord" (Luke 2:11). And another just last week: "For what does it profit a man to gain the whole world and forfeit his soul?" (Mark 8:36).

They'd met at church, and she was happy to see that his faith appeared to run deeper than Sunday morning Christianity. That was one major plus for him.

* * *

The next morning, Trey stretched in bed. He'd let others see way more than he intended last night, but he was surprised by the reaction of the women. They seemed to really respect how far he had come on his own, especially given his background. He couldn't ever remember somebody actually feeling proud of him for accomplishing something. If someone had, he or she had never expressed it to him.

He felt for both Sophia and Grace.

Sophia was clearly still in love with this Greg guy from her past, but she wasn't willing to admit it. He could see it in the way she sighed when they asked her more questions about Greg and their history together.

And Grace just wanted her old husband back—not the *Dooms-*

day Preppers version who was convinced the world was going to end soon. She seemed fearful to express her feelings to Harold, and Trey couldn't blame her. How could she even live with that man?

Trey considered the exchanges he'd had with Harold yesterday and wondered if maybe he should back off the old man today. Harold had his views, but Trey sort of admired Harold's convictions. He disagreed with them, but at least he had them. So many people today didn't seem to care about what was going on politically.

Trey glanced at the time on his phone. It was just after eight-thirty. He needed to jump into the shower if he was going to make it to breakfast by nine o'clock. Alma seemed like the grandmotherly type who might get all up in his business if he didn't show up on time.

Alma appeared to run a tight ship, but he liked her. He never had a chance to meet his grandparents. But knowing Alma gave him a sense of what having a grandmother would've felt like. She's the type who would've fixed Thanksgiving dinner every year, encouraged sleepovers with cousins, and took her grandkids to the park on Saturday afternoons.

That was so far from Trey's experience. He'd asked his parents about his grandparents, but both were estranged from their parents to the point that they were no longer even in contact. His grandparents could be dead by now, for all he knew. Maybe he should make a point of trying to find them when he got back. Maybe one or two of them were still alive.

He jumped into the shower, thinking this trip might turn out to be a good decision after all. He wouldn't find a girl, but maybe he'd make a couple of new friends. He needed that in the worst way. But they wouldn't really be true friends, would they?

Sophia lived in Atlanta. Grace lived in Kansas City. And Alma lived here. They almost couldn't be more spread out across the country—especially since he was in Portland. And it's not like they were going to be trading texts.

By the time he turned off the faucet, he'd nearly changed his mind about this trip. But it was Christmas Eve now. *Why not just see what happens?* If he toned things down with Harold, the tensions would ease.

What none of them knew was, Christmas Eve was also his birthday. Yet another way he had been shortchanged in the past. When his parents were actually trying to be good parents during his childhood, they often gave him one gift, saying it was for both holidays. He realized now that he should've been happy to receive any gift, but it never sat right with him. Probably because they didn't even acknowledge his birthday with a party or by making him his favorite food.

"It's just another day," his dad would slur. "You should be thankful for what you've got."

Meanwhile, his mom shrugged every time his father said it—a common reaction for her. He hated seeing anybody shrug now. For him, it symbolized indifference and he couldn't understand or respect indifference and apathy. A person might as well be dead inside. That was something he promised to never allow to occur in his own life. He'd always voice his opinions and stand for what he thought was right. If he ruffled a few feathers along the way, well, it was better than shrugging. At least they would know where he stood. On second thought, maybe he wouldn't back down from Harold for the sake of peace.

Chapter 7

Grace gripped the steering wheel, fearful of the two-inch base of snow that'd built up on Highway 17 overnight. They only had a short twenty-minute drive to Antonito, but she never liked driving on snow, even though she'd seen her share of it over the years in Kansas City.

"Hopefully, you'll like this place better." Grace tried to keep the edge out of her voice, but she wasn't succeeding. "It's called Steam Train Hotel, and it's in nearby Antonito. The website says it's 'the hotel with an inn touch,' but there won't be any festivities like at Mercy Inn. It'll just be you and me."

"Perfect."

The front tires slipped a bit and Grace jerked the wheel in response, almost losing control of the car. She took her foot off the accelerator, slowing to forty-five miles per hour—the speed she planned to maintain for the rest of the trip. "This highway is in terrible condition, Harold. And you know I'm not a good driver on snow. I wish we could've stayed at Mercy Inn."

"We'll be fine. Take your time. It's not that far."

"I really liked Ray and Alma. Sophia and Trey too."

Harold scoffed. "We'll have a quieter Christmas now, and that's all I care about." He fussed with the radio, saying he was trying to find a station with old Christmas carols. At least he had a little Christmas spirit.

"I still need to call Alma and tell her we checked out this morning. She's going to be so disappointed."

"They run a business. They aren't disappointed over such things—except over the loss of revenue."

"But they'd already bought gifts for both of us. She went to a lot of trouble in preparing for our stay." Grace used her glove to wipe the fog off the windshield in front of her. The defroster hadn't gotten warm enough yet to do so.

"Don't try to guilt-trip me into going back. Please call Alma and tell her about our change of plan."

A car approached on the other side of the highway. Grace could barely see its oncoming headlights. "I'll call her when we arrive. Unless you want to call her now?"

"I'll pass."

The other car got bigger and seemed to lose control momentarily, turning at a slight angle. Grace pulled over to the shoulder so the oncoming car had plenty of room. The driver regained control and passed them without incident.

Grace eased back onto Highway 17. "I'm a nervous wreck driving in these conditions, Harold."

"You're doing fine. We'll be there soon. Start looking for a sign that says Antonito. It shouldn't be that much farther."

She glanced in her rearview mirror and winced. "Oh, no! That car we passed just spun off the road and ended up in the ditch. We need to turn around and help them."

Harold groaned. Clearly, he wasn't happy about her decision, but what was he going to say? He'd sound like an ogre if he objected too much.

By the time Grace pulled onto the shoulder behind the car and stepped out with Harold, the two passengers were already out examining the damage.

"Is everybody okay?" Harold buttoned his coat and slipped on his gloves.

"We're fine," said a man who appeared to be in his mid-forties. "Think the radiator is broken though. We hit the embankment pretty hard." He popped the hood to take a look.

"Thanks for stopping." A woman extended her hand toward Grace, then Harold. "My name is Jennifer. This is Sam."

"Pleased to meet you," Grace said. "These roads are terrible, aren't they?"

Sam spoke up, still under the hood. "We're not going anywhere this morning without a tow. The radiator is leaking fluid everywhere." A green pool was already forming in the snow under the car.

"Where were you headed?" Harold rubbed his hands together.

"Just up the road, to a place called Mercy Inn."

Grace laughed.

"You guys know it?" Sam said.

"We just came from there," Grace said. "I thought Alma said she wasn't expecting any more guests over the next couple of days. Does she know you're coming?"

"You know Alma?" Jennifer patted her hands together. "Small world. She's expecting us, but we're not guests. We're from a church in Antonito, and she asked us to provide background music during the Christmas holiday. She's always got something special planned for guests."

"Well, I'll be," Harold said.

"Mind giving us a lift back to Mercy Inn?" Sam said.

* * *

Alma raised her eyebrows when Harold and Grace walked in with Sam and Jennifer. They must've shown up at the same time.

"Good timing, everyone," Alma said. "Breakfast is ready. Help yourselves. It's buffet style."

Jennifer pulled Alma aside while the other three dug into the food. "We should probably tell you that we got into an accident. Nobody was hurt. But the roads are awful. Only a little snow has fallen, but it's made the highway extremely slick."

"Oh, mercy."

Jennifer yanked her stocking cap off, and her long curly auburn-colored hair fell down her back. "Your guests were kind enough to pick us up. We piled our gear into their trunk."

"I don't understand."

"They were headed east on Highway 17," Jennifer said.

"Why would they be out on the roads at all?"

Jennifer shrugged. "They didn't say. But they both seemed pretty tense."

"I'll go talk to them, dear. Are you sure everybody is okay? How much damage is there to your car?"

Jennifer filled her in on the details. As she was doing so, Alma got a fuller picture. Harold and Grace were checking out and going to another nearby inn. She was sure of it.

"I have a feeling that your accident was not really an accident." Alma looked up in time to see Ray headed toward them. "I'll explain more later."

"If you'll toss me your keys, I'll bring in your equipment while you grab a little breakfast." Ray held out his hands, ready to catch them.

"You'll have to ask Harold or Grace. It's their car."

Ray raised an eyebrow.

"I'll explain shortly, dear. For now, can you ask Harold and Grace for their keys?"

Ray nodded and headed in their direction.

Alma glanced into the breakfast nook, pleased to at least see Sophia and Trey sharing a table. Grace stood nearby, chatting with both of them. Harold hid behind her.

"You can run, but you cannot hide," she whispered. Apparently, the Taylors were really supposed to be here. She couldn't wait to see their eyes when they opened their gifts.

* * *

Ray helped Sam bring in the musical equipment, setting it near the Christmas tree in the living room. Memories of Sarah Rose's impromptu concert from a couple of years ago ran through Ray's mind. It'd been Sarah's reawakening, of sorts. Sam and Jennifer hadn't played at the inn for several years, so Ray was looking forward to hearing them again. *The Father often uses music to heal.*

Harold lurked behind his wife. Ray sensed he better strike up a conversation or they might be gone. Harold was volatile, especially after last night. He could take off at any moment.

Ray placed a hand on Harold's shoulder and greeted him. "Grab yourself some breakfast. Alma always makes too much."

Harold eyed the heaping bins that were piled with scrambled eggs, bacon, and sausage patties before giving in to the temptation. "Don't mind if I do, thanks."

Ray followed him, picking up a plate and looking for a way to ease into a conversation without setting Harold off. "Today

49

will go better than last night. I have a good feeling about it."

"It would go much better if Trey weren't here. He knows exactly how to push all my buttons." Harold piled his plate full, finishing it off with a couple of pieces of French toast and syrup.

"Go easy on him, okay? You heard his story. He doesn't have anybody he can count on. Be the bigger man and let his comments slide. Look for his heart. It's buried under the sarcasm and cynicism. I think you'll find a scared young man who's lost his way or maybe one who's never found it."

The two of them grabbed a table together without saying anything else. Ray took Harold's lack of response as a good thing—like maybe he was considering what he'd said. Of course, he might just be ignoring him.

Chapter 8

Harold cut a sausage patty in half, stabbed a piece with his fork, and shoved it into his mouth. He didn't owe Ray anything. He had to admit though, Ray's words made him think about his own upbringing. His parents were certainly more responsible than Trey's, but they were far from perfect. They provided for him and his siblings just fine, but they were from a generation who believed children were supposed to be seen, not heard.

Looking back, he never really knew his dad. He worked in a factory in Kansas City his entire life. He often came home covered in soot, reeking of sweat. And he was never in the mood to talk. He kicked off his shoes by the door, tucked the newspaper under his arm, and settled in his recliner where he often fell asleep until dinner was served.

Harold's mom also fell short. She performed all the duties of a good mother and wife, but she grumbled often. The two seemed to have an unspoken agreement—each would perform his or her duties for the family, but they didn't have to pretend to be happy about it. Harold always found that to be disconcerting, and it always made him wonder if taking care of responsibilities was all there is to life.

After he married Grace, he only spoke to his parents a few

times a year—mostly on holidays, and nobody seemed all that upset about it. Including him. From his perspective, it was probably because he had Grace by his side. And they really did have many good years before she started showing her negative side. He suspected she was just reacting to his newfound interest in politics and the way he spoke about where the country was headed. But a man couldn't help what he was passionate about, could he? Besides, he wanted to make sure his children and his grandchildren had a decent country to grow up in.

What might his life have looked like if he hadn't married Grace at such a young age? Would it have looked like Trey's? He wouldn't have allowed that to happen, but drifting is the natural order if you aren't disciplined, especially when you're young and have no idea how to make a plan and then stick to it.

He sighed. Could he really be the bigger man, as Ray suggested? He glanced up at Ray, who was going to town on his food, shoveling it in quicker than Harold. Thankfully, Ray wasn't the chatty type. He gave a man room to think without constantly pressuring him. Harold admired that about him.

"How have you stayed under 300 pounds?" Harold asked Ray. "Has Alma been cooking like this your entire married life?"

"She goes all out for the holidays."

"I'll say." He paused for a few seconds and lowered his head. "You know, we really hadn't planned on coming back this morning."

"I figured that was a possibility. What changed your mind?"

"A car accident."

Ray raised his eyebrows.

"You already left? And got into a car accident?"

Harold filled him in on the details.

"I'm so glad everybody is okay," Ray said. "But it seems as if you were meant to be here for the holidays."

"If you're saying God arranged this, I'm not buying it. I'm as religious as the next guy, but I have my doubts that God would actually cause two good people to spin off the road just to make sure I changed my mind about leaving."

"Stranger things have happened, my friend," Ray said.

The hair on the back of Harold's neck stood on end.

* * *

Trey entered the lodge a little later than he'd planned. The aroma of freshly-cooked breakfast was calling his name.

"There's the birthday boy!" Alma said.

How does she know? I didn't share that information on the website when I registered. At least, not the I can remember.

Alma patted her hands. "A little birdie told me. Don't you worry one bit. I made sure to pick up separate gifts for your birthday and Christmas. I've never been a believer in buying one gift for two celebrations."

"I don't understand."

"There's nothing to understand, dear. Just enjoy it."

This was downright creepy. Had she visited one of his social media accounts? That had to be it. But he had everything set to private. And he hadn't accepted any new friend requests recently. *Bizarre.*

"Grab yourself a plate, dear. We'll be meeting in the living room in about fifteen minutes to begin our activities for the day."

"I hope one of those activities involves going outside for a look around this property. It's so beautiful." Trey nodded out the window.

"You'll have plenty of free time to go exploring."

By the time he poured himself a cup of coffee and filled his plate, Sophia and Grace were just about to get up, but when they saw him coming, they waved him over and sat back down. Harold was sitting with them, but he wasn't waving. In fact, he wasn't even acknowledging that Trey existed.

Trey took the remaining open seat and greeted the two women before turning toward Harold. "And how are you today?"

"Peachy. You?"

"Couldn't be better."

Grace and Sophia were just finishing their conversation—something about fabric. Apparently, Sophia had always wanted to learn how to sew, and Grace was an expert seamstress, so she was dropping her knowledge all over Sophia.

"Did you get a good night's rest?" Grace asked Trey.

"Better than I expected. This place is so relaxing. I started a fire in my fireplace last night and fell asleep to the crackling noises. How about you? Sleep well?" He took a couple of bites and washed it down with his coffee. He thought he detected a slight frown on Grace's face, but as soon as he spotted it, it disappeared.

"We were a bit restless last night, but when we finally fell asleep, we slept well." Grace patted Harold's arm.

Sophia flipped her hair over her shoulder. "What do you guys think Alma has planned for us today? Her secrecy is killing me. One part of me expects a traditional Christmas celebration from her, and the other part has a feeling it'll be something bigger." Sophia made eye contact with Trey.

"Yeah, I have no idea." Trey focused on his plate instead of the question. He wasn't sure he wanted to know. Alma had already made him feel uncomfortable. Who knows what else she'd dug up on all of them. On second thought, Harold wouldn't like that one bit. Seeing his reaction could be fun.

A few minutes later, Trey took the final few bites of his food, just as Alma was calling them to the living room. Everybody took the same seats they were in the previous day.

"We're happy to let you know that Sam and Jennifer will be providing live background music for us." Ray pointed in their direction in the corner, and they bowed slightly. They haven't been with us for a few years, so we're thrilled to have them back."

"And we're happy to be back." Jennifer took a seat on a stool and began to play a Christmas song on her guitar that Trey didn't recognize. Sam followed her on the keyboards. It wasn't too loud, making for the perfect background noise—even if it wasn't Trey's style of music.

Alma rocked back and forth in her chair. "Ray and I know it's a little unorthodox to be opening Christmas presents on Christmas Eve morning, but that's just how things worked out. We picked up some gifts for you and we want you to open them old-fashioned style—one at a time. And after you have opened one, we want you to hold it up for all to see so we can ooh and ahh over it."

Ray took Alma's hand. "Don't let her fool any of you. I didn't have a single thing to do with any of the gifts you see over there." He gestured toward the tree. "This was all Alma."

Alma blushed. "Not entirely true. He helped with a couple of them."

Trey had never actually seen anyone blush.

"Ray has a surprise up his sleeve for later too," Alma said.

"Can we get a volunteer to hand out the gifts?"

"Oh, I'd love to do that," Grace said. "That used to be my job when I was a little girl."

"Perfect, dear. Go over to the tree and find a triangular-shaped gift that's propped against the wall. It'll have Sophia's name on it."

* * *

Sophia's stomach fluttered as Grace found her gift and handed it to her. She took her time to unwrap it. "How in the world did you have time to buy and wrap all of these gifts, Alma? And you actually wrapped them, rather than shoving them in a gift bag, like I typically do."

"Oh, time isn't really a problem for me, dear." Alma rocked back and forth, appearing to be as content as a person could be.

Sophia ripped the wrapping paper far enough to see what was inside, and her breath caught in her throat. "A flag display case? How did you ..." Tears trickled out of her eyes and flowed down her face as she pulled off the rest of the wrapping paper and ran her hand over the case's smooth cherry wood finish. She dug for a tissue in her purse, thankful for a reason not to have to look up into everybody's faces.

"What's the significance, Sophia?" Grace asked.

Sophia sighed and bit her lip, trying to gather her thoughts. "My dad died in 1999. I was so young." She paused. "At the funeral, my mom wanted me to have the flag that's always issued to the spouse of the deceased. I have it in my bedroom, and I treasure it. But I've just never gotten around to buying one of these cases so I could display it properly. And honestly, part of me just wasn't ready to do so. It made his death seem so ..." Sophia looked at Alma. "How did you know?"

"I didn't, dear."

"But, I mean—how did you know what to buy?"

Ray cut in. "She seems to have a sixth sense when it comes to gift buying—and in dealing with people in general." He patted Alma on the hand. "That means I've never been able to get away with anything in our marriage. She always calls me on it."

Sophia chuckled but shifted in her seat. This was such a specific gift.

"Tell us more about your dad," Alma said.

Christmas had been her dad's favorite time of year, which is one of the reasons she missed him so much at this time every year.

"He was a beautiful contradiction." Sophia ran her hands along the sides of her slacks. "He was a traditionalist when it comes to Christmas, but a nonconformist for other holidays, like Valentine's Day. He always said there was no reason to have a special celebration on February 14, since every day was Valentine's Day with my mother. And he really did treat her that way."

"As if Christmas hasn't been commercialized," Trey said.

"Like I said, he was a beautiful contradiction."

"What else can you tell us about him?" Grace said.

Sophia smiled and wiped her eyes. "He was regimented. He liked to read the newspaper at the same time every evening. And yet, he was fun. He'd drop anything he was doing at any time if my sister or I wanted to perform a fashion show for him, or if we wanted to paint his fingernails."

"Sounds like a great dad," Alma said.

"He was as perfect as they come. I don't mean that he didn't have flaws or make mistakes, but he couldn't have been more attentive to Mom or us." She paused for a few seconds. She looked into everyone's eyes, wondering if she should go on, but feeling compelled to.

"The day he had a massive stroke ... well, it was devastating. He slipped into eternity later that night." She fought back her tears more successfully than she would've imagined.

"Until this very minute, I hadn't realized that I've never really gotten over his death. I think that's why I never purchased a display case for the flag. If I kept putting it off, then I'd always have something else I needed to do for him."

"That makes sense," Grace said.

Sophia rubbed her hands over the case. "But this ... it feels like the beginning stages of closure." She wept.

Chapter 9

Grace pulled Sophia close to let her cry on her shoulder and the inn grew silent, except for Sophia's soft cries. When the tears finally stopped, Sophia pulled back.

"That's been a long time coming," Sophia said. "I'm so embarrassed that it happened here though. Forgive me."

"Dear, breakthroughs like yours are the reason this place exists." Alma's warm tone was like salve to Sophia's hurting heart. "You're among friends here. Who better to grieve with?"

"Thank you," Sophia whispered, then wiped her eyes. "Enough about me. Whose turn is it?"

"Grace, your gift is next," Alma said. "It's the green rectangular-shaped one with snowflakes on the wrapping paper."

"How do you remember such things?" Grace said.

"It's one of her many hidden talents," Ray said.

Sam and Jennifer began playing the instrumental version of "God Bless Ye Merry Gentlemen."

Grace hummed along as she looked for and found her gift before taking her seat. She didn't want for much. Her life was mostly wrapped up in Harold's wants and desires. She was just trying to be the best wife possible. But as she pulled the wrapping paper off the box, an old dream fluttered back to life deep down inside her.

"It's a laptop computer?" Grace's eyes grew wide. "This is too much."

"I got a great deal."

As a retired school teacher and former librarian, Grace had always dreamed about writing novels, but she'd never had the time. "I'll use it to begin writing once Harold and I are settled into our new place here in Colorado."

"You're a writer now?" Harold raised his unkempt eyebrows.

"I always wanted to be one. I'll certainly have the time once we find a new home."

"Where abouts in Colorado?" Ray asked.

Snowball reappeared. He sought out Harold and jumped into his lap. He curled up and closed his eyes.

"Somewhere around here—in the southern part," Grace said. "We're looking for something out of the way, maybe even off the grid. We want to get back to the simple pleasures of life."

"Tell us more about your desire to write, dear." Alma rocked back and forth in her chair.

"When I was a librarian, I devoured all of the *Little House on the Prairie* books, and prairie romances, and historical romances. In those books, there was a certain respect for the way things used to be, and I always thought that when I retired, I'd like to write those kinds of books—if there's anybody still interested in reading them."

"I think it's a great idea." Harold's encouragement stunned her. "I didn't even know you wanted to be a writer, but like you said, you'll have time once we get settled in. You should go for it."

Grace looked at her lap. "But I don't know the first thing about writing a good book."

"That's what Amazon is for," Trey said. "Just buy a few books about the topic, and maybe take an online course or two from a successful author in your genre, and you'll be good to go."

"You make it sound so easy." Grace bit her lower lip.

"If you combine your passion with information and knowledge, you'll be set," Trey said. "You can do it."

Grace reached for Harold's hand, and they locked fingers. His grip was less tense than normal. He might not be getting along with Trey, but clearly, he respected Trey's show of support for his wife. That was a start.

Grace felt her confidence grow in that instant. Maybe Trey was right. And with Harold's support, maybe she really would have something to look forward to every day. She envisioned getting up at the crack of dawn, firing up the coffee maker, and settling in for a couple of hours to write in her own breakfast nook where she'd get to see wildlife and the seasons change. It sounded heavenly.

"Thanks, Trey," Grace said. "And thank you, Ray and Alma. This is an amazing gift." *How in the world can they afford to give away such an item? It costs more than our room fee for our entire stay.* It didn't make sense—especially when she looked at the remaining stack of gifts under the tree. Was this some sort of reality show or something? One in which a hidden millionaire gives away a bunch of money or gifts?

"It's our pleasure, dear. Mercy Inn is often a place where people come to find a new path or to rediscover old ones."

Grace exhaled. "Well, you've certainly done that for me."

"What do you say about handing out the next gift?" Alma asked.

"Who's next?" Grace said.

"Harold, dear."

* * *

Harold had been supportive of Grace's dream when she revealed it a few moments ago, but he felt unsettled about the circumstances surrounding the gift. It was like Ray and Alma—her, especially—knew their guests before they even arrived. *How?*

Alma instructed Grace about which gifts to retrieve next. Grace handed Harold a box the size of a toaster and one that was maybe half that size. The commotion was too much for Snowball, so he jumped out of Harold's lap and curled up by the fireplace. Harold unwrapped the first gift and just stared at it. He didn't know the first thing about a ham radio. He flipped the box over to read what it had to say, hoping to buy a little more time to come up with a reaction.

Ray came to the rescue. "Most people who live remotely have a ham radio since they are too far from most emergency responders. So, folks in this part of the state look out for one another. If a fire breaks out, they find out via ham radio and everyone comes running. If someone gets injured, the same principle applies."

Harold nodded. "Makes sense. Thanks. I'll put this to good use."

"It's a great way to connect with people and to get to know your neighbors—even if they are spread out."

Harold nodded his appreciation, even though getting to know his neighbors wasn't at the top of his priority list. He could see why it would be important to do though.

A memory flashed through his mind. He was maybe seventeen years old, sitting in the car next to his uncle on a summer business trip from Kansas City to Oklahoma City. CB radios were just beginning to become popular at the time. His uncle had just picked one up, and he showed Harold how to use it.

"You have to come up with a handle," his uncle told him.

"What's that?"

"It's like a code name, and it's the way you will identify yourself when you talk to people."

"I want to be Warpaint."

"That works."

The CB radio sprang to life in front of him. "Breaker-Breaker 1-9, this here is Midnight Cowboy. I'm making a run to O-K-C and looking for a little conversation to keep me awake. Anybody got a copy?"

Harold's uncle grabbed the microphone from its holder and keyed it. "Roger, Midnight Cowboy. I've got a copy. This here is Traveling Salesman, come on."

Over the next thirty minutes, the two men held a conversation and Harold found it fascinating. How could two strangers hit it off so well?

"Can I try?" Harold asked.

His uncle handed him the microphone. "This here is Warpaint. I'm the nephew of Traveling Salesman. You still out there, Midnight Cowboy?"

"Roger, Warpaint. Nice to meet you. Is your handle based on the Kansas City Chiefs horse mascot? Over."

"It sure is."

"Far out. I can't talk much about football, but I'm a huge baseball fan. How about you? Over."

"I'm a Royals fan, all the way."

"Looks like you're going to have quite a team this year, Warpaint. You've got Big John Mayberry, Cookie Rojas, Lou Piniella, Jerry May, Bob Oliver . . . and who else? Over."

"Don't forget Paul Splittorff, Steve Busby, and Al Fitzmorris."

"Copy that. You're going to be tough to beat. Hope they make a run at the pennant. Over."

Midnight Cowboy turned out to be a Yankees fan, which, for a Royals fan, couldn't be any worse. But he was nice, and after that conversation, Harold couldn't wait to get into the car with his dad to seek out conversations with other people—especially people his age.

The CB radio expanded his world exponentially, and it made him more aware of what he'd been missing. In fact, he could trace his global and national awareness back to those moments in the car with his uncle, chatting on the CB.

"Yes, a ham radio is the perfect gift," Harold said to Ray and Alma. "Thank you so much." He opened the second gift to find a Blue Yeti USB microphone.

"That's one of the most popular microphones for podcasting," Ray said. "If you're interested, you can start your own podcast. This microphone can be plugged right into your phone. I've included the cable you'll need to connect the microphone."

Harold caught Grace rolling her eyes. He wished she wouldn't embarrass him like that in front of everybody. Didn't she know how much it hurt him? Truth be told, he'd been considering starting a podcast to talk about his political views for some time. Once they got settled into their new place, it would be the perfect time to start one.

* * *

Alma indicated that Trey was next. She whispered something

to Ray, who excused himself and disappeared. "Today is Trey's birthday," Alma announced. "So, he gets two gifts!"

"Your birthday is on Christmas Eve?" Sophia asked. "That doesn't seem fair."

"You play the cards you're dealt."

"Well, happy birthday!" Sophia took a sip of her coffee. "I'm glad you're here to celebrate it with us."

Trey wasn't accustomed to receiving many gifts. He wasn't even accustomed to people acknowledging his birthday. And he was still a bit creeped out by the fact that he didn't know how Alma found out that it was his birthday in the first place.

He started with the gift in birthday cake wrapping paper—a small box that didn't weigh much. He shook it, and it rattled. Anxious to find out what was inside, he tore into the package and found two keys on a keyring. Underneath was a small card. He read it aloud. "You will need these for your 2017 Piaggio Typhoon 50 scooter."

"What?"

He had priced these back in Portland because his car was dying and he couldn't afford anything else to get to and from work. He also wanted to leave a smaller environmental footprint. But these things ran $2,000. What was going on?

"You can choose another model or color if you don't like the one Ray chose, dear."

"This model is perfect! And the color doesn't matter to me. But how—"

"Oh, and here's the scooter." She pointed toward Ray, who had just walked back inside, wheeling the blue scooter toward the seating area. "Actually, the dealership was nice enough to allow us to use this one to present to you. It's one they use for test drives. Ray arranged for you to pick up your actual scooter at a dealership in Portland once you get back. It'll be the same year, model, and color, right dear?"

"You betcha," Ray said.

Trey sprang out of his seat. Amazingly, the scooter even had a helmet that was hanging from one of its handlebars. How would Ray know what size helmet to get? Somehow, Trey knew it would fit.

He made eye contact with Ray, who seemed as happy as a man could be, and then with Alma, who was still seated in her rocking chair.

"Happy birthday, dear. Now, open your Christmas gift."

It was too much for Trey to take in. Who were these people? And why did they seem to care so much about him?

Ray activated the kickstand, allowing the scooter to stand on its own in the lobby before he joined Trey, who had just returned to his seat.

"That is the nicest thing anybody has ever done for me," Trey said. "My car is on its last legs, and I had no idea what I was going to do."

"Aww, we're glad you like it, dear."

His Christmas gift box was bigger and heavier. He didn't shake this package. He was afraid to, knowing it might very well contain something expensive. He peeled the wrapping paper off and lifted the lid on the box. It was software of some sort.

"Wait ... you bought me Photoshop, InDesign, and Adobe Illustrator? I have no words."

"Why is this software significant, Trey?" Sophia asked.

"I've been thinking about launching my own graphic design business. I scrimped and saved for a new laptop a while back—one that would be powerful enough to run all of this software, but I haven't been able to afford any of these programs."

Trey's eyes met Alma's. This was no coincidence. Neither were any of the other gifts. But none of it made any sense.

"These are such thoughtful gifts. They really are, but how do you know so much about all of us?" Trey waved his hand around the room. "I never told anybody I was looking at these scooters, and nobody knows me well enough to know I needed this software. What's going on?" He stared at Ray and Alma, expecting an answer.

"I'm a praying woman, dear. When I heard that the four of you would be joining us for Christmas this year, I simply asked the Father to help me select the perfect gifts for everybody. You're confirming that he answered my prayers."

Chapter 10

After the group stopped for a break, Sophia stepped inside the bathroom located just off the lodge's living room and locked the door. Memories of her father's death came rushing back. He was too young to die. But as a doctor, she knew death was no respecter of age. She'd delivered news to many young patients of their impending demise and was often struck by how cruel life could be.

Just last month, she had to tell two new parents that their infant had a malignant brainstem glioma—a high-grade, fast-growing brain tumor that forms in the tissue of the brainstem. In this baby's case, cancer had already spread too far to stop it. The look on her parents' faces when she delivered the awful news nearly crushed Sophia. Against all medical advice, she hugged them and wept with them. The baby died several weeks later.

But it was different when it was your own father. He'd had a massive stroke and died within a few hours at the age of fifty-eight. She'd always been her daddy's little girl. He'd taken her to the circus when she was young because she saw one on television and shown an interest. He took her fishing every Saturday during the summer when she was ten, and she'd squealed with delight every time she caught a fish. Meanwhile, he had the biggest grin on his face as he was taking her fish off the hook.

Even as a teenager, when other girls her age were pulling away from their fathers, she clung to hers, asking him for advice about boys, school, and even her hair. It's not that her mother wasn't around and available. And it's not that she wasn't a good mom. For some reason, she just felt closer to her dad. She felt safe with him.

Sophia closed a bathroom stall door, hoping to further shield herself from the outside world. She took a seat and buried her face in her hands. Her dad had been gone eighteen years, and she still wasn't ready to let him go. She wept for the years they'd lost, for the advice she'd never get from him again, and for the void she felt without him in her life. The full weight of her loss crashed down on her.

Twenty minutes later, she unlatched the stall and approached the sink. Her makeup had streaked down her face. Thankfully, she had her purse with her. After making herself look presentable again, she returned to the living room only to find that everybody had migrated to the nook.

* * *

Grace wasn't sure why she'd never bought her own laptop to start writing. They certainly had the money for it. But something about the idea seemed too far-fetched, and she always wondered what Harold might say. Besides, she wasn't exactly tech-savvy. She wasn't sure how she'd even learn to use the new machine, but somehow, receiving the laptop from Ray and Alma made her feel like she was supposed to begin writing.

For years, she'd had one particular story in her mind about a woman who decided to stay home and help her widowed father on the ranch, rather than getting married and having children. It probably wasn't the most unique idea when it came to prairie romances, but she felt like she could bring that woman to life. Not that Grace was like that character, but she did know how it felt to sacrifice for someone you loved.

"Mind if I sit here?" Sophia asked.

"Of course not. Pull up a seat."

Harold and Ray were chatting by the front door, pointing at something outside, and Trey had disappeared after they had opened gifts.

Sophia sniffed the air a couple of times. "Alma's cooking smells like my momma's. I can't believe I'm hungry again."

"This is my second cup of Christmas Delight already, so temporary indulgence must go hand in hand with this place," Grace said. "Either that, or we're all just weak."

Sophia laughed, despite her puffy eyes.

"Want to talk about it?" Grace took a sip of her coffee.

Sophia dabbed around her eyes. "I've just never fully accepted my dad's death—until I opened that flag display case this morning."

"Your relationship was obviously special."

"He was always my rock. The one who had time for me. The one who would drop anything and listen to me go on and on about boys, my dream of becoming a doctor, and just stupid teenage drama."

Grace didn't miss the fact that Sophia wasn't talking about her mother, but it seemed like her father had played both roles. "I think he'd be proud of you."

"What makes you say that?"

"You fulfilled your dream of becoming a doctor. But more than that, you're someone who cares about other people. That would make any parent proud."

"Thank you for saying that." They sat in silence for a few seconds before Sophia spoke again. "Tell me more about your dream of becoming a novelist."

"The main characters for my first book have been occupying space in my head for years."

"What has stopped you in the past?" Sophia leaned back against her seat, crossed her legs, and began to dangle her shoe.

For Grace to admit that she feared Harold's response, especially after she'd just learned he was all for her writing, made her feel crunchy. She'd once had a friend who used that word to describe the feeling a person gets when she realizes she might have caused someone else to be embarrassed. She thought the word was perfect for this situation.

"I'm a cautious person by nature." Grace hoped that Sophia would buy her fib, but when Sophia tilted her head, she knew Sophia wasn't buying it. "Part of my fear comes from not wanting to go toe to toe with Harold. He's changed in recent years. Become angry at the world."

Sophia stopped dangling her shoe. "Has he mistreated you?"

"No, no. Nothing like that. I just wasn't sure how he'd react to me wanting to do something for myself. I realize now that my fears were unwarranted."

Sophia's foot began bouncing up and down again. "It sounds like you've got a novel to write."

Grace smiled. Just hearing someone say that felt like a charge to do so.

Alma set a ham the size of Chicago on a table in the nook.

Smoke rose from the food and twirled toward the ceiling. Grace wasn't ordinarily a ham person, but she had a feeling she was about to make an exception.

* * *

"So, how aware of the mountains do we need to be when choosing a new place to live if we want to make sure the radio will get a good signal?" Harold asked Ray, gazing out the front door of the inn.

"Ham radios—or 'amateur radios,' as some people call them—do have some issues with reception in mountainous regions. We get pretty good reception here at the inn and the surrounding area. But I can't speak for anything outside of maybe a ten-mile radius."

Harold nodded. "Any suggestions in general for getting the best reception possible?"

"You can choose a place near a mountaintop, or one that sits in a valley between mountains. Or you can choose a town close to a repeater. Pagosa Springs has one. It's maybe 80 miles west of here, and it's on the other side of the mountain range. Durango has one too. It's approximately 140 miles west. And there's one in Silverton, which is 180 miles northwest. The only other one I know about in southern Colorado is in Cortez, which is in the southwest corner of the state."

"Can you jot that information down for me? I'll never remember it."

"Sure thing." Ray grabbed a pad and paper from the front desk, scribbled everything he'd just told Harold, tore off the page, and handed it to him.

"I feel like you've opened up a whole new world to me. Thank you. Say, I'm wondering if a handyman can find work in this area."

"Is that what you want to do once you're settled?"

"I'm thinking about it. I can fix about anything."

"It'll take a while to build up a clientele, but I suspect you'll have more work than you really want within a year. Word of mouth spreads pretty quickly. The best way to do it is to go into town and mingle a little. Get to know your neighbors. Your services will gradually come up in conversation. Some of the businesses also have bulletin boards where you can pin flyers and business cards."

Harold could at least take advantage of the bulletin boards. The last thing he wanted to do was mingle. But he didn't really want to admit that to Ray. He had something else on his mind right now anyway. As happy as Harold was to receive the ham radio, it seemed too tailored to him, making him suspicious. Neither Ray nor Alma would've known Harold and Grace were considering a move to Colorado before they'd arrived. And from the sound of things, everybody else's gift was too specific too.

* * *

Trey climbed off the scooter and hung his helmet on the handlebars. He did a three-sixty around the bike again. He couldn't believe this was his. Portland probably wasn't the ideal place to operate a scooter since it rained so often, but it rarely got below the forties in the winter and snow was rare. And it'd be much better and cheaper than buying another car.

As he approached the door to the inn, he saw Harold and Ray in conversation just inside. He eased the door open and the two men stepped aside.

"Take your new scooter for a spin?" Ray said.

"I did, but I didn't get far. The highway was too snowy, so I turned around and came back."

"What'd you think?"

Trey took a step closer. "It's the most incredible gift anybody has ever given me. I don't even know what to say." Before he could speak, Ray wrapped him in a hug and it felt like the most natural thing in the world. He had no idea what motivated Ray and Alma, but he'd never forget them.

Ray pulled away and patted Trey on the back. "You just said all you need to say. We're glad you like it."

"I love it."

Harold turned and walked away. Was he jealous that Trey's gift cost more money than his? Or was something else going on? Trey had no clue, but he wasn't going to allow Harold to spoil the moment.

"How did you guys know I needed transportation?"

"Well, we knew that you were from Portland, where the cost of living is high and that you were young. Alma took it from there. She figured that if you already had a reliable vehicle, you'd still enjoy taking the scooter out for a Sunday drive every now and then."

"A Sunday drive?"

Ray patted him on the shoulder. "Forgive me. It's an old expression from an old man. It just means taking a leisurely drive—the way people use to do after church services on Sundays when they didn't seem to have a care in the world."

"Sounds very 1950ish."

"Indeed."

* * *

"Dinner is ready." Alma waved her hand toward the spread on the table in the nook. "Go ahead and dig in, everyone." The guests stood but hesitated, so Alma took charge. "Grace, why don't you go first? Everyone else can follow."

Grace obliged, picking up a plate with gold trim. "Alma, this looks incredible." Grace stabbed a piece of ham with the serving fork and set it on her plate.

"I enjoy cooking, dear. I wouldn't know what to do with myself if I didn't go all out for the holidays."

Harold followed Grace while Sophia and Trey chatted in line behind them. Trey was fitting in better than yesterday, but Harold seemed as distant as ever, even after his brief conversation with Ray by the door. Just as Alma was beginning to offer up a silent prayer for wisdom, Harold dropped his partially-filled plate onto the floor, splattering food in every direction.

Harold winced. "I can't believe I just did that. I'm so sorry." He grabbed some napkins from the table, got down on his knees, and began to clean up.

"Don't worry about it, dear. I'll have this taken care of in a jiffy. Just grab a new plate and start again."

Alma opened the supply closet behind the front desk and pulled out a broom, dustpan, mop, and bucket. She made quick work of the cleanup and then filled her own plate so she could join everyone in conversation.

A few minutes later, she slid into a seat at Harold and Grace's table. She'd hoped all four of their guests would be sitting together by now, but the tension between Harold and Trey was too high.

As Sophia and Trey ate and talked at the next table, Harold lowered one of his eyebrows and seemed to be on the verge of asking a question, but he hesitated. Alma gave him the room he needed. She'd learned a long time ago to not press. Some people need time to process. Although, she had her doubts that Harold was one of them. He seemed to know exactly what he wanted to say at all times. Maybe he was considering Grace's feelings before he spoke. If so, that was progress.

Alma nodded toward Grace. "Mind sharing anything more about the idea for your novel? Or is it top secret?"

"Did you ever read *Christy* by Catherine Marshall? Or maybe you saw the television series that was adapted from the novel?"

"I loved both." Alma hoped Grace was planning to write something similar.

Grace nodded. "Me too! And how about the *When Calls the Heart?* series that's currently on the Hallmark Channel?"

"One of my favorites."

"Okay, so I have this idea for a series of novels set in the Smoky Mountains around that same era. Maybe the 1910s. As I said, they'd be about a woman who decides to stay on the homestead to help her father, rather than getting married and moving away, but then he dies unexpectedly. She decides to stay on the homestead and work it, even though that was nearly unheard of back in those days."

"Does she have a suitor?"

"She has two! One who loves her and would treat her well,

but she doesn't have romantic feelings for him—at least, not yet. And another who seems more interested in the homestead than her, but she loves him with all her heart."

Alma took a sip of her coffee. "I know which one I'm rooting for already."

"The problem is, her homestead isn't producing enough income or food for her to survive. It'd been in trouble before her father passed away. Now, it was even worse. So, she feels like she has to choose between survival and love. What she doesn't realize is, she might be able to have both."

"You have to write that story, dear. I'll be the first one to buy a copy."

Chapter 11

Sam and Jennifer played the instrumental version of "Angels We Have Heard on High" as background music in the living room while everyone continued with lunch in the nook. For Sophia, the music changed the mood in the room. Or maybe just *her* mood changed.

If Trey had noticed her puffy eyes, he hadn't said anything so far. He returned to their table with a second plate full of food and took a seat. Sophia shoved her food around with her fork, not really feeling much like eating after coming to terms with the loss of her father. *Maybe I should focus on something else.*

"So, you were looking at scooters recently?" she asked.

Trey stopped shoveling his food in momentarily. "I've been eying that particular scooter for nearly a year. Can't tell you how many times I've test-driven one. But none of those test drives felt as good as the trip I just took, you know?"

"Ray and Alma are extremely generous people. I can hardly believe the gifts they got us."

"Sort of makes me feel bad that I received the most expensive one."

Sophia leaned forward. "I think all of us got exactly what we needed."

Trey pointed at her and nodded. "It's almost too good to be

true."

"Haven't you learned any manners whatsoever, boy?" Harold said from his table just a couple of feet away. "Don't point at folks. It's rude."

"Just because I don't go by some archaic set of rules you grew up with doesn't mean I don't have any manners."

Sophia held up her hand. "It's fine, Harold. Really. He meant no harm."

Obviously, Grace wasn't making any headway when it came to defusing this situation between Harold and Trey. Sophia thought about giving it a shot herself but doubted she'd have any chance of getting through to Harold.

"It doesn't matter if he meant harm or not. Somebody needs to teach him how to behave."

Trey rolled his eyes, prompting Harold to stand up and clench his fists. To Trey's credit, he remained seated.

Grace grabbed Harold by the arm. "Sit down. Now."

To Sophia's surprise, he obeyed. *Good for Grace.* It was the most backbone she'd shown since they'd gotten there, and it was just in the nick of time.

* * *

Harold's face grew hot as he slid back into his seat. Grace had embarrassed him again. Why did she feel the need to treat him like a child? He'd been supportive of her desire to begin writing. Why couldn't she back him on this? Trey was clearly in the wrong. Someone needed to call him on it.

And why hadn't Trey even stood when he'd been confronted?

Men in Harold's era wouldn't have hesitated to do so if someone else challenged them. The old order was dying. Harold had sensed it for a long time, but being around Trey the past couple of days confirmed it. This country had no chance of surviving with the likes of Trey running it one day.

"What were you thinking?" Grace whispered.

Harold didn't answer. He didn't feel like he needed to. Instead, he took a bite of his potatoes and stared at his plate. His time for talking was over.

A few minutes later, Alma announced it was time to finish lunch and head over to the living room to pick up where they'd left off with that ridiculous Nicebreaker game. Early on, Ray and Alma said the guests didn't have to participate in any of the activities if they didn't want to, so he'd take them up on it and see if they'd be true to their word. He considered heading back to the room right then, but he wanted to make a statement with his silence.

After they took their seats in the living room, Alma spoke up. "All right, Harold. Why don't you get us started for round two."

Harold folded his arms. "I'm going to sit this round out. I don't want to play. So, nobody ask me any questions."

"Harold, honey." Grace touched his arm.

He pulled away from her.

"Come on. It'll be fun."

"I'm out."

"Grace, dear? Why don't you get us started, then?"

* * *

Jennifer played the instrumental version of "God Rest Ye, Merry Gentleman" on the keyboards. She had it set to a volume that was low enough to not be distracting—at least in Trey's opinion.

"I choose Trey." Grace flipped her index card. "If you didn't end up marrying your first love from high school, what happened to cause your breakup, and was it the right decision for both of you?"

Trey took a deep breath. Being vulnerable in front of Harold would lead to mockery. Trey was sure of it. But he'd answer the question anyway because he liked to talk about Hannah.

"When I was fifteen, a new family moved into our neighborhood, three doors down from us. The day they moved in, I was reading a book on the front porch. It was a hot, sticky July day. I glanced up and made eye contact with the most beautiful girl I'd ever seen. She was helping her family carry the boxes inside. As soon as we locked eyes, my eyes darted back to the page, but I couldn't focus, so I risked a second look. She smiled and I knew I was in trouble."

"Sounds like love at first sight," Sophia said.

"I don't know if I believe in that or not, but the spark was there with Hannah from that very first minute. I found the courage to set my book down and approach her."

"This is getting good, dear." Alma rubbed her hands together. Harold rolled his eyes.

"I introduced myself to her parents and then her, offering to help them get everything inside."

"Sounds like someone had an ulterior motive," Harold said.

Grace backhanded Harold across his arm. "I think it's romantic."

Trey kept going. "When Hannah and I shook hands for the first time that day, I actually felt a shock run up my arm."

"Oh, brother," Harold said.

"We spent the remainder of the summer together. She was fifteen, too, so neither of us could drive, but we were within walking distance of plenty of hot spots. We took a walk one night and she wanted me to take her to the coolest non-chain coffee shop I knew about."

Trey's stomach flipped as he recalled that day. "I knew just the place to take her: Palio Espresso and Dessert House. On the way there, she asked me if there were any shelters for the homeless in the area. Her family had volunteered at one in Chicago."

"There are several," I told her. "I read an article about the Portland Rescue Mission recently. People who are down on their luck get more than just a hot meal there. The place also offers career planning, job searches, showers, clothing, mail service, transitional housing facilities, and spiritual guidance for those who want it."

"Her eyes got big and she asked if they needed volunteers. That's when I learned she had a giant heart. It's also when I realized mine was too small.

"I pulled out my cell phone and called them right then. The woman I talked to invited us to come down and explore the opportunities. We visited the next night and discovered that they ask volunteers to commit to a minimum of one year of service because they have a desire to be highly relational, which made total sense."

"I love that," Alma said.

"We did too. But it also felt like a big commitment, to me at least. To Hannah, not so much. From the very start, she made me want to be a better person."

"That's so sweet, dear. So, did you sign up for a year?"

"A boy will do anything for a girl, even when he's just fifteen."

"Did you ever make it to the coffee shop that night?" Grace asked.

Trey nodded. "And Hannah loved it. She said the rectangular-shaped walnut tables, high-backed wooden chairs, and soft lights make the place look like a library."

"That's probably why I love it so much," I told her. "Are you familiar with Donald Miller?"

"*Blue Like Jazz* is one of the most influential books I've ever read. Second only to his *A Million Miles in a Thousand Years*."

"He stops in here on occasion when he gets back to Portland."

"No way! Have you ever met him?"

"I've seen him here a couple of times, but I've never approached him."

"You have more control than I do."

Trey shook his head at the memory of that summer. "I know they say that opposites attract. In my case, I couldn't have found anybody more similar in tastes."

"Are you still together, dear?"

Trey shook his head. "We were victims of circumstance. Her dad's company transferred the family to the east coast eighteen months later. We video chatted every day for a while, but one day she seemed distant."

"Another guy?" Harold's tone almost sounded hopeful.

"Like I said, we were victims of circumstance. No teenage romance survives 3,000 miles of distance for long."

Sam picked up an acoustic guitar and began to strum the opening chords of "Hark! The Herald Angels Sing." Nobody said anything for a few seconds, seeming to take in the music.

Finally, Alma asked the question that Trey knew was probably on everybody's mind.

"Are you still in touch?" The way she methodically rocked back and forth in her chair was calming.

Trey set his head back against the chair and looked toward the ceiling. "We still text every now and then."

Ray reached for Alma's hand. "Is she with somebody else?"

"She was ... for a while. But not the last time I talked to her."

Sophia raised her eyebrows. "How much time do you have off work for the Christmas holiday?"

Trey could see where this was going. "We're closed 'til January 2."

"So you have a full week after you leave here," Sophia said. "Maybe you should pay her a visit."

Trey hadn't answered the follow-up question that Alma had originally asked him about whether the breakup was the right decision for both of them. The truth was, they hadn't made a decision to break up. Hannah's family moved away and that made the decision for them. It didn't seem fair. And it certainly didn't feel like the right decision to Trey. But when you're fifteen, you're sort of powerless in a situation like that.

Sophia did have a point. He wasn't powerless now. It wasn't the first time he'd considered visiting Hannah, but money was always so tight. He had enough cash in his pocket now though. What would be the harm in paying Hannah a visit?

Trey nodded in response to Sophia's suggestion. "I'll think about it."

* * *

"Sophia, it's your turn to ask the next question, dear."

"Grace, this one is for you." Sophia flipped her next card and read the question. "Do you believe in soul mates? Why or why not?"

"That's a new question," Alma said. "Must be from one of our guests last year."

Grace nodded as she tried to gather her thoughts about such a heady topic. "You'd think an old married lady like me would say she believes in soul mates, but I'm just not sure I can wrap my head around the idea. How many billion people are there on earth? I mean, if a young person believed in soul mates and waited to date and marry that person, he or she might be waiting forever."

"How did you know that Harold was the one for you?" Sophia asked. "Did he feel like your soul mate?"

"After our third date, Harold brought me back to my house, and Mom invited him inside. I guess she wanted to get to know him better if we were going to keep dating. Well, she brought out the photo album and embarrassed me to death, showing Harold my baby pictures—I was a rather chubby baby, and then progressing through my grade school years. It was awful."

"I didn't think it was awful," Harold said. "I really wanted to know more about you, and that helped."

"I don't know why Mom did this, but after she closed the photo album, she got us some iced tea and brought out a charm bracelet. I'd never seen it before, but it was beautiful. It had charms depicting the Eiffel Tower, a gondola, the Leaning Tower of Pisa, Big Ben, Stone Henge, the Coliseum in Rome, and several other places."

"These were the stops that your grandparents made on their honeymoon," Mom said. "Grandma gave it to me when I was about your age. She told me to make my own memories. To dream big. To find the man who made me happy. She said my journey didn't need to mirror hers. I loved that so much that I decided to wear this bracelet until I found my own true love. I guess I should've given this to you a year or two ago, but now that you're dating, it's certainly time to pass it on to you."

"My face grew hot since Harold was sitting right there," Grace said. "I wondered if he'd feel the pressure to live up to such a legacy. And, like I said, we were only on our third date. But Mom must've seen something in him, even at such a young age. People tended to marry much younger back then. I have to say, her act gave me confidence in Harold and me. But Harold's response sealed the deal for me."

"Oh, do tell, dear. What'd he do?"

All eyes turned toward Harold, who shrugged. "All I did, if I recall correctly, was to ask to see the bracelet. And I began to ask questions about Grace's grandmother, and how she'd gotten so wise. Most adults I knew wanted their children to relive the way they'd done things. So I was intrigued by the matriarch who'd given her daughter so much freedom."

"And that's when I knew Harold was the guy for me," Grace said. "So it wasn't a mystical experience that led me to him or made me believe we were meant to be together from the beginning. It was spending time together and growing closer through experiences, and then seeing how much he really cared about me and my family that made all the difference."

"I cared about your family because they produced you."

"Aww, that's sweet, dear."

Grace nodded, happy to have found the Harold she fell in love with all those years ago—even if for a moment. She leaned over and kissed him.

Chapter 12

Alma indicated that it was Trey's turn to choose someone for his next question. He picked Alma and flipped his card. "What is your philosophy about food?"

"Oh, that's such a good question, dear. And it's another new one." Alma glanced toward the ceiling. One of the corners of her mouth went up. "My philosophy about food is that it's so much more than nutrients. The term 'breaking bread' can be found in the Bible in Acts 2:42, where it says believers in the first century 'devoted themselves to the apostles' teaching and the fellowship, to the breaking of bread and the prayers.'"

As Alma spoke, she tried to read the room. Tensions still felt high between Harold and Trey, although, Harold had just shown a side she'd been waiting to see. But Harold wasn't the only problem. Trey enjoyed provoking him.

Trey tilted his head sideways when Alma made eye contact with him, as if to try to figure out what Alma was thinking. In reality, Alma had stopped thinking and started praying for a solution to the growing feud between Harold and Trey.

"Sharing a meal means sharing the details of life with one another," Alma continued. "And, more importantly, it means being vulnerable. You've heard it said that the way to a man's heart is through his stomach. I believe that to be a universal truth, regardless of gender. Food brings people closer. It's one of the reasons I love to cook. And it's one of the reasons Ray and I provide all the meals for our guests each year. We believe in the power of sharing a meal."

Trey nodded. "That's a pretty good philosophy. I'm glad I didn't get that question. I probably would've said I eat because it tastes good."

Alma laughed.

* * *

Jennifer picked up her acoustic guitar and began to strum the opening chords of "Deck the Halls," setting a festive mood while Sam browsed the snack table.

Sophia loved everything about this place. She hadn't realized how tense she'd been when she arrived. Practicing medicine was so rewarding, but it also operated in a high-stress environment.

"I believe it's Ray's turn," Alma said.

He chose Sophia for his next question. "1 Corinthians 7:7 says each person has his own gift from God. What is your gift and how are you using it right now to help others?"

Sophia tapped her fist against her lips for a few seconds. "My church offered a spiritual gifts class a couple of years ago and all of us took a test. My results revealed that I had the gift of service, but that's always bugged me because as we studied each gift, I remember the gift of service primarily being done behind the scenes—like a deacon might perform. And I have no idea what that is supposed to look like for me."

Alma gently rocked back and forth. "The gift of service allows for a pretty broad range of actions, though, dear—at least in my understanding. Don't you believe your work as a doctor qualifies as service?"

Sophia opened her mouth for a second, then closed it. "I just have a sense that I'm not doing everything I should be."

"If you're supposed to be doing more, dear, or maybe something different, you'll figure it out. In fact, I have a feeling that you'll know before you leave here."

She had the sense that Alma was right, but hearing Alma say it gave her pause. Ray and Alma's gifts, insights, and comments like the one Alma had just made convinced Sophia that something spiritual was happening here—something deeper than she'd ever experienced.

* * *

"Here's the last question of this round," Alma said. "We can stop and take a break after this. Trey, this one's for you." She flipped her next index card. "What is your favorite book, and why?"

"This is an easy one. After Hannah mentioned Donald Miller's *A Million Miles in a Thousand Years*, I had to read it. I'd read *Blue Like Jazz*, but not this one. *A Million Miles* changed my outlook on risk."

"How so?" Ray asked.

"It's about choosing to live a better story." Trey paused for a few seconds to think of an example from the book. "For Miller, finding a better story started by getting off the couch to engage life. He took a bike ride across America. He hiked the Inca Trail in Peru. He pursued a woman. He put down the remote control and his routines long enough to take chances—to explore."

"Sounds wise," Ray said.

Trey nodded. "He began living as if he were a protagonist in a novel who wanted something, faced obstacles, got shot down, and got up again before facing a major decision. In a novel, you expect the main character to go after what he wants because living without it is not acceptable. Most of us don't live that way because we're afraid, so we settle."

The room was quiet.

"At one point in the book, Miller says, 'Part of me wonders if our stories aren't being stolen by the easy life.' I don't think I'll ever forget that line."

"What do you think he meant by that?" Ray asked.

"He gave a pretty good example by referring to a friend named Jason, I think. His teenage daughter was into smoking pot and dating a guy who wasn't good for her. As Jason told Miller about this, Miller said, 'She's not living a very good story. She's caught up in a bad one.' A couple of months later, when the two men spoke again, everything had changed."

"How so, dear?"

"Jason couldn't sleep the night after his conversation with Miller as he thought about the story his daughter was living. He came to the conclusion that he hadn't shown his daughter any other role to play. In fact, he hadn't mapped out a story for his family. And so his daughter chose an easy story."

Everyone nodded.

"Jason began looking for a better story. He found one when he read about an organization that builds orphanages around the world, and he suggested they do the same. His wife and daughter weren't crazy about the idea at first, but after sleeping on it, his wife—who'd been distant from Jason for a while—came into the kitchen, put her arms around him, and told him she was proud of him."

Sophia's eyes got big. "I love that!"

"It gets better," Trey said. "A few days later, their daughter came into their bedroom and asked if they could go to Mexico to build an orphanage. Their daughter ended up crawling in bed between Jason and his wife like she did when she was little."

"Is that why you decided to travel by yourself this Christmas, dear? Because you want to live a better story?" Alma's tone and gentle style had a way of making Trey feel at ease.

"I guess I'm still trying to figure out what that might look like for me. I know it's about more than choosing a good career, or buying a nice house, or getting married, or even traveling here for the sake of it."

He thought Hannah might be part of the equation. She inspired him to live for causes bigger than himself, like serving people at the homeless shelter. It gave him meaning and purpose, and it was one of the many reasons he really needed to reconnect with her.

"I might find that answer to that question if I spend some time with Hannah."

"Does this mean you've decided to visit her after you leave here?" Sophia could barely contain a smile.

"If she wants me to, it does."

* * *

Alma announced that it was time for a break and that snacks were available in the nook. Harold excused himself, saying he wanted to go back to his cabin and take a nap, and Trey decided to head outside to explore the area. That left Sophia and Grace to chat among themselves at a table in the nook.

Ray believed it was time for a powwow, so he waved Sam, Jennifer, and Alma over to the reception area, where they gathered behind the front desk.

"Thanks for the music," Ray said. "Live music really adds a nice touch."

"Glad to be here," Jennifer said. "So, what's your assignment? What's going on?"

"We have an elderly couple who are at odds," Ray said. "Harold has his eyes set too firmly on the things of this world. He's frightened by the cultural changes he sees and he's become bitter. You may have even picked up on that when you rescued them."

Sam nodded. "He was pretty quiet on the trip back to the inn. But yeah, that's tough."

"And his wife wants to spread her wings as a writer, but for some reason, she'd never shared that with Harold."

"She was probably afraid of how he might react—like it was impractical or something," Jennifer said.

Alma agreed. "We also have a doctor who wants more out of her life but isn't sure where to find it. And we have a young man who isn't close to anybody and seems to be drifting through life."

"Throw in the fact that this is our final year here and I can't help but think something big is going to happen," Ray said. "I just don't know what that might be."

"Let's pray, dear."

The four of them joined hands, bowed their heads, and boldly approached the throne of grace.

* * *

Harold stepped into his cabin and pulled out his phone. He needed to check the news to find out what was going on in the world, and he wanted to visit some real estate websites for property near the ham radio repeaters that Ray had mentioned. And the truth be told, Harold was still ticked at Grace. He needed to get away from her for a while.

The first news website he visited on his laptop announced that there'd been a shooting at a big box store where a last-minute shopper lost his marbles. Harold shook his head. *A man shot three people over a television. This world has lost its ever-loving mind.* He went to his favorite political website and saw a headline about 65% of Americans not saving anything out of their paychecks. Another headline proclaimed that a celebrity had received a letter from a woman who had changed her name to a symbol and was encouraging the celebrity to run for president.

On and on it went. Bad news. Lack of preparation. An insane fascination with celebrities. And most sites were still buzzing about a mass shooting that'd taken place the week prior. *This country really has lost its way. The only hope at this point is to find a place far away from everyone else and then to protect it at all costs.*

He pulled out the sheet of paper Ray had given him that listed the cities with repeaters nearby and began to browse the web for the perfect property. Nothing was available in Pagosa Springs,

Durango, or Silverton, but two properties were for sale in Cortez. He brought up the City Data page and learned that the city had nearly 9,000 residents and the crime rates weren't terrible. The median age of residents was nearly 40, which was a tad young for him, but at least it was above the millennial cutoff point. Both places he was considering were more than ten miles outside of the city.

One, in particular, caught his eye. It was a small cabin tucked back in the woods, and it had all of the amenities he wanted. Best of all, according to the description, the nearest house was over three miles away. Grace could go into town for groceries, or to church, or to meet with friends, but they would still be far enough from the dangers that came with living in the city. He'd run the place by Grace later tonight.

He bookmarked the page on his phone, satisfied that he made some progress. Knowing he had some time to kill before dinner, he considered going for a walk but it was too cold for that. Instead, he turned on the television and laid down on the bed. The next thing he knew, Grace was shaking him, telling him to wake up.

"Come on, Harold. It's time for dinner. Alma has outdone herself again."

Harold rolled out of bed, trying to get his bearings, and headed for the bathroom. "Let me wash up. I'll be ready in a minute."

"I'm going to change into a nicer blouse since it's Christmas Eve. You missed an entire round of Nicebreaker. We had so much fun."

"Sounds like it worked out for everyone, then," Harold said from the bathroom. "You enjoyed each other's company and I got to sleep."

"I think you should give everyone another chance, Harold.

These are good people. Even Trey. You heard his story. He's dealing with a lot. And he's been by himself for so long. He needs supportive people around him."

Harold leaned over the sink and splashed cold water on his face. He had to admit, hearing about Trey's upbringing and then about him losing the love of his young life made Trey seem less entitled. But he still rubbed Harold the wrong way.

"Ray and Alma gave us the option of not playing the game," Harold said. "I'm not sure why it's such a big deal that I took them up on it."

Grace appeared in the bathroom doorway, buttoning her blouse. "That option is for people who are hurting—whose story is too difficult for them to share in front of people who might judge them. Much like you've been doing to Trey, but he told us his story anyway."

She's taking someone else's side again. Harold rolled his eyes and shook his head, unwilling to say anything else. He couldn't win with Grace. There was no sense in even trying.

Chapter 13

Sophia couldn't get her last Nicebreaker question out of her mind. *What is your gift and how are you using it right now to help others?* Why was this bothering her so much? She entered the lodge. Sam and Jennifer waved her over to the nook. Sophia didn't need any more caffeine for the day, so she poured a glass of ice water and joined them at their table. She got a glimpse out the window and noticed that snow had just begun to fall again, drifting slowly toward the ground.

"You're certainly more disciplined than I am." Jennifer nodded toward Sophia's glass of water. "I always drink way too much coffee when I'm here."

"I'll be bouncing off the walls if I don't slow down," Sophia said. "Besides, I usually advise my patients to partake of everything in moderation. I sort of need to practice what I preach, right?"

Jennifer smiled. "How long have you been practicing medicine?"

"Six years. But it feels much longer. How about you? How long have you and Sam been performing?"

"It feels like an eternity." Jennifer cut her eyes in Sam's direction. "We've been playing together since we were kids."

"Oh, really? Are you a couple? Or just friends?" Sophia stole a glance at Jennifer's ring finger, noting that it was empty.

"We're more like brother and sister," Jennifer said.

Sam put his arm around Jennifer and squeezed her shoulder, as if to emphasize the point. But from Sophia's perspective, it almost felt like they were trying too hard to convince her. But she knew from experience that relationships could be quite complicated.

"Do you tour?" Sophia asked.

"We mostly play at retirement homes, graduation parties, birthday parties, and coffee shops around the southern part of the state. Occasionally, we venture out farther, but we always seem to have enough work within a couple of hundred-mile radius."

"Have you ever wanted more?"

Sam cleared his throat. "We see this as a ministry. That's not a slight against artists who are focusing on the business aspect. We've just always believed that music is supposed to be a ministry for us, and without fail, people are touched by it, no matter where we play."

"That must be satisfying," Sophia said.

"Everybody's different," Sam said. "Some should be touring and reaching the masses. Others are supposed to be playing locally and touching people there. As long as you're doing what you're supposed to be doing, it's extremely satisfying."

Sophia bit her lower lip. "How do you know what you're supposed to be doing? I mean, is it trial and error? Or do you base it on how people respond?"

"Something tells me you're struggling with this issue yourself." Jennifer touched Sophia's arm.

"You could say that."

"Are you wondering if you should move your practice?"

97

Jennifer asked.

"It's not really that. I'm just unsettled, restless."

"That's usually a pretty good indicator that you need to keep your options open," Sam said.

Jennifer nodded in agreement. "Care to share more?"

"I don't really know anymore."

"Sam and I will pray for you. Can we do so now?"

"Certainly. Thank you."

They bowed their heads and joined hands.

"Lord, you know Sophia's heart," Jennifer started. "You know that she wants to glorify you by serving the least of these, but she's uncertain about how to do so. She's unsettled, Lord. And you often cause a holy unsettling in the spirit of your people when you want them to seek a different path. Show her the way, Father."

"Abba, Father," Sam prayed, "thank you for giving each believer a unique calling on his or her life. Thank you for gifting Sophia in the manner that you have. Thank you for giving her a heart for service. Speak to her heart today. She's listening for your voice. Offer her clear direction."

The three of them squeezed hands and broke the circle.

"I can't thank you enough for your prayers," Sophia said.

"We're happy to do it," Jennifer said.

As they parted, a feeling settled in Sophia's spirit—one she needed to explore further.

* * *

Lying on his bed in his cabin, Trey stared at his phone. He'd brought up Hannah's name in his contacts a few minutes ago, but he couldn't bring himself to text her. Seven years had passed since their relationship ended. Wouldn't reaching out to her now seem desperate? But it's not like they hadn't traded texts since breaking up. They had done so here and there. He wished he'd kept in better touch but when he sensed that she was pulling away, his ego decided it would be better to let her go.

He'd been in two relationships since things ended with Hannah. One of them, Kristina, probably wasn't his best decision. She was fun and outgoing, but she also didn't know when to stop. She loved to party and when she was drunk, she flirted with other guys. Eventually, he heard she'd done more than flirt. He met the other woman, Ashley, at work a year and a half ago and they started hanging out right away. Since they were both technology geeks, they hit several trade shows together. She was far more low-key than Kristina, but she wasn't looking for anything serious. Eventually, he learned why. She'd never gotten over her previous boyfriend.

Against his better judgment, he opened a text message window and began to type: "Hey, Hannah, how u been? What r u up to these days?" He hit send. And waited. He shook his head. She'd see right through him. Know that he'd want to reconnect. But it was the truth. Might as well be open about it. If she responded favorably, he'd offer to visit after leaving the inn in a couple of days—no matter where she was living now, assuming she wasn't with somebody. That seemed like a pretty big assumption.

He laid his head back down on his pillow, opened his music app, and hit play. The first song was "Whatever It Takes" by Imagine Dragons. It wouldn't have been his first pick, but he'd found his share of new jams this way. A couple of minutes into the song, Trey's phone chirped, causing his stomach to flip.

"Hey, Trey. It's been a minute since we talked. How are you?"

He stared at the screen, not wanting to respond too quickly. Besides, he never knew how to answer that question.

"I'm okay. Been thinking bout u." He couldn't concentrate with the music on, so he turned it off.

"Been thinking about you too."

"So, what's new? U been hangin out with anybody?"

"Nah. Not for a while now. You?"

"Not for a year. Where u living?"

"I moved to Austin for an internship last year."

"What sorta internship?"

"With a publishing company."

"I shoulda known u'd end up in publishing."

"Yeah, books are my life."

"Cool."

"How about you? Where are you living and working?"

"Work for a small graphic design company in Portland. Pay is decent. I've got no complaints."

"Nice. You off for the holidays?"

"I am. Currently in New Mexico. Long story. Maybe I can share it with ya soon?"

"I'd like that."

"Hey, I have next week off from work. What do u think about me coming to see ya day after tomorrow?"

"Really? How long can you stay?"

"A few days. If u want."

"I'd love that."

"Cool. Text me ur addy."

* * *

Harold and Grace entered the lodge and sat down for dinner. Someone had pushed two tables together so all eight people could share their meals together. Grace was happy just to get Harold to come back. After he'd ditched the Nicebreaker game earlier that afternoon, she'd had her doubts. He hadn't even put up a fight. But he also hadn't said much when she'd asked him to come back to the lodge for dinner.

Trey seemed to be in an especially good mood. Had he reconnected with Hannah? That was Grace's guess. Very little made a man happier than to receive a favorable response from the woman he loves. And Trey clearly loved Hannah.

"Harold, could you please pass the rolls and butter?" Trey said. They were sitting directly across from one another—certainly not by choice. Harold and Grace had taken the final two seats. Grace suspected that Ray or Alma was behind it, hoping they could work things out.

"Here you go." Harold didn't have an edge in his voice. In fact, he didn't seem to have any life in his voice. That concerned Grace. She'd seen him shut down in the past and this was the tone he used. But at least he wasn't being contentious. They'd be finished here at the inn soon enough and would be searching for new property and a new life the day after next. Maybe that's what Harold was thinking about.

"Thank you." Trey had a slight grin on his face as he received the items from Harold.

"Did you get some rest, Harold?" Alma asked.

"Yeah, thanks for asking."

"You missed a great round of Nicebreaker, dear. I hope you'll join us for the next round after dinner."

"I'm opting out, Alma. But thanks for the invitation. I may join you though and just not participate."

That was progress. Usually, when Harold was in shut down mode, he pulled away from everybody. Maybe he was in observation mode. She'd seen that from him a time or two. It usually happened when he was suspicious of someone. But why would he be suspicious of anybody here?

* * *

After dinner, they moved into the lodge's living room. Despite what he'd said at dinner, Harold considered going back to the cabin. But he didn't want Grace to think he didn't care about her or the others. She should know better by now, but her eyes told him she thought he was being anti-social. He needed to process everything that had happened so far. But he seemed to be alone in that sentiment, given that the room was buzzing with conversation.

Ray held up his hand. "Excuse me, everybody. Usually, on Christmas Eve, I like to read the Christmas story from Luke 2. If it doesn't offend anybody, I'd like to read it now for you."

Nobody objected. So he began.

In those days a decree went out from Caesar Augustus that all the world should be registered. This was the first registration when Quirinius was governor of Syria. And all went to be registered, each to his own town. And Joseph also went up from Galilee, from the town of Nazareth, to Judea, to the city of David, which is called Bethlehem, because he was of the house and lineage of David, to be registered with Mary, his betrothed, who was with child. And while they were there, the time came for her to give birth. And she gave birth to her firstborn son and wrapped him in swaddling cloths and laid him in a manger, because there was no place for them in the inn.

And in the same region there were shepherds out in the field, keeping watch over their flock by night. And an angel of the Lord appeared to them, and the glory of the Lord shone around them, and they were filled with great fear. And the angel said to them, "Fear not, for behold, I bring you good news of great joy that will be for all the people. For unto you is born this day in the city of David a Savior, who is Christ the Lord. And this will be a sign for you: you will find a baby wrapped in swaddling cloths and lying in a manger." And suddenly there was with the angel a multitude of the heavenly host praising God and saying, "Glory to God in the highest, and on earth peace among those with whom he is pleased!"

Nobody said a word for a few seconds. Then, as if on cue, Sam began singing "Away in a Manger" while Jennifer strummed along on her guitar.

Away in a manger, no crib for a bed,
The little Lord Jesus laid down His sweet head.
The stars in the sky looked down where He lay,
The little Lord Jesus, asleep on the hay.

The cattle are lowing, the Baby awakes,
But little Lord Jesus, no crying He makes;
I love Thee, Lord Jesus, look down from the sky
And stay by my cradle till morning is nigh.

Be near me, Lord Jesus, I ask Thee to stay
Close by me forever, and love me, I pray;
Bless all the dear children in Thy tender care,
And fit us for Heaven to live with Thee there.

The experience was as close to church as Harold had experienced in a long time.

* * *

Over the next hour, they worked their way through another round of Nicebreaker. From Ray's perspective, most of the charges were making great progress. Trey seemed to be on track. Sophia was on the verge of a breakthrough. He could just feel it. And Grace already seemed to have found what she needed. But Harold was going to be more difficult. He hardly seemed to be paying attention during this round. To his credit, though, he was there by Grace's side.

Alma stood. "Okay, everyone. Let's stop for a little break. Feel free to grab some snacks or refill your mug and chat for a bit. Then you're in for a treat. Sam and Jennifer are going to perform for you tonight. They can play almost any Christmas song you know, so it'll be an all-request show. Be thinking about some of your favorites during the break."

Chapter 14

Sophia caught up with Jennifer during the break. "Thanks for praying with me earlier. I really needed that."

"Happy to do it. Feel any better?" Jennifer set her guitar in the stand next to her.

"I feel expectant. Something about this place makes me believe that heaven is near. I know that sounds silly." Sophia paused. "My faith runs hot and cold—more cold lately. I can't really put a finger on why. Does that ever happen to you?"

"Knowing the Father's will can be difficult, but it's not meant to be so. In our limited understanding, I think we often try to work things out and then ask God to get involved. In reality, he expects us to wait on him—to trust him. Not in a passive way though. Waiting means to leave the details to him while we go about the work he's put in front of us."

Sophia nodded. "That's the clearest presentation of under-standing God's will I've ever heard." As comforting as it was, it also furthered Sophia's belief that more was happening here than met the eye.

* * *

Trey took a seat by himself in the nook and pulled out his phone to text Hannah, then thought better of it. He didn't want to seem too eager. Just when he set his phone down, it chimed with a text from Hannah.

"What'cha doing?"

"Relaxing. U?"

"Thinking about your trip 2 Austin. I'm sorta nervous."

"Shouldn't we be past that?"

"Aren't you nervous?"

"In a good way, I guess."

"How so?"

"Just looking forward 2 seeing u."

As much as he loved to text with her, he wasn't going to tell her he hoped they'd get back together, especially before they had a chance to hang out. It would happen naturally if it was supposed to.

"Me too. Okay, I'll let u get back to your Christmas celebration."

"Merry Christmas, Hannah."

"And merry Christmas to you."

Trey flipped his phone face down and set it on the table.

"Penny for your thoughts." Sophia startled him.

"Take a seat, if you want." Trey waved in the direction of the chair across from him.

She pulled out the chair and sat down. "You looked deep in thought."

"I'm texting with Hannah. It stirs up all sorts of emotions I haven't felt in ... well, since the last time we were together."

"That makes me so happy." Sophia leaned back in her chair. "Obviously, she means a lot to you."

"I don't think I realized how much until that stupid game

reminded me."

"Maybe it's not so stupid after all."

"Maybe."

"Want to tell me what you're thinking?"

The corner of Trey's mouth curled downward. "I'm thinking I could be setting myself up for pain. I mean, she's agreed to see me. I'm planning to visit her as soon as I leave here. But ..."

"You're afraid the spark might not be there anymore." Sophia tapped her fingers on the table. "Or that she won't be interested. Or that she'll be different somehow."

"It's kinda hard not to think all three."

"It's a risk, for sure. But isn't she worth it?"

He nodded.

"What do you have to lose? If you visit her and things are different between you, then you're free to move on."

"That's just it. I've never had a spark with anyone else. I'm afraid to take the risk because if it doesn't work out, it feels like my one shot at love is gone."

"You're getting way ahead of yourself. You guys had a natural attraction back in the day and you were just being yourselves. So, just be yourself when you visit her and see what happens."

"Good point. But now I feel like I know too much. I've had a taste of what love feels like. Before Hannah, I didn't have a clue. And after her, nobody else has come close to making me feel the way she does."

"That's why I'm proud of you for reaching out to her and setting up a trip. You've got a second chance at love, Trey. Embrace it."

He bit his lower lip. "Thanks. I'll do that."

* * *

When Sophia got back to her cabin that evening after the concert, she reached for her cell phone to call Sarah Rose. Sarah had asked her to touch base if she decided to go to Mercy Inn because she wanted to hear how Ray and Alma were doing. Since Sarah had been here before, maybe she could explain what Sophia was feeling about the place.

"Sophia?" Sarah picked up on the second ring. "I'm so glad you called. Does this mean you decided to spend the holidays at Mercy Inn?"

"I'm here as we speak." Sophia laid down on the couch and propped her head on a pillow. "Everything you said about the place was dead on. It's stunning, and Ray and Alma are the best hosts imaginable."

"How are they doing? Does she still make a coffee concoction called 'Christmas Delight?'"

"They are doing great, and yes. Love that stuff."

"Me too."

"Are you home for the holidays?" Sophia put her hand on her forehead.

"Just for a few days, then we're headed right back out on the road again."

"Great. I hope you're resting your voice." Sophia paused, not sure how to ask the question that was on her mind.

"What's up, Sophia? I can hear hesitation in your voice."

"I need to ask you something about Ray and Alma."

"Sure thing."

"Did they seem like they knew too much about you while you were here?"

"Alma is certainly intuitive, if that's what you mean."

"It's more than that. She went out and bought all of us Christmas gifts and they met our exact needs—needs nobody could've possibly known about."

"That's a bit strange, but like I said, she's intuitive—especially when it comes to meeting the needs of others."

"Okay, well ... I'm just going to say what I'm thinking, even though you're going to think I'm crazy." Sophia closed her eyes, squeezed her forehead, and gave voice to her suspicion. "I think they're angels."

Silence.

"Angels who run an inn in the most obscure, out-of-the-way place in America?"

"What better place?"

"I've got nothing."

"Are you a woman of faith, Sarah?"

"I am."

Sophia sat up, reached for her Bible on the coffee table, and flipped it open. "Then you've read Hebrews 13:1-2, right? Mind if I read it?"

"Not at all."

"Let brotherly love continue. Do not neglect to show hospitality to strangers, for thereby some have entertained angels unawares."

Silence.

Sophia put her Bible back on the coffee table. "What if the angels are the ones who are doing the entertaining in this case? Isn't that conceivable?"

"I've never even considered it," Sarah said. "But it gives me chills just thinking about it."

"They just sort of have a presence, you know. And what

about the name of the place? It sounds like a heavenly hospital, doesn't it?"

"My assistant is tech-savvy. Why don't I put her to work to see what she can find out about the history of the place? I'll be in touch tomorrow evening, if not sooner."

Sophia thanked her, ended the call, and laid back down on the couch to think and pray. If Ray and Alma were angels, they didn't appear to want anybody to know it. They had been hosting people over the holidays like this for decades from the way it sounded. Why wouldn't they want to be found out? Apparently, God had other plans in mind.

Who was she to rock the boat? And she didn't sense that Harold, Grace, or Trey were believers, so she suspected she'd only hear laughter from them if she voiced her opinion. Well, maybe Grace would be open to the idea. But something about blowing the whistle on Ray and Alma just felt off. She'd need to pray long and hard before she took another step.

As she began to pray, her mind wandered back to the ambiguous answers Ray and Alma had provided, and the gifts that matched so perfectly that it would've been creepy if they weren't sent from heaven. And Alma had mentioned that she was a praying woman. *Lord, how am I supposed to handle this? Should I say anything to anybody else?*

* * *

Harold still wasn't saying much by the time they got back to their cabin. Grace doubted her ability to get him to open up, but she decided to give it a try.

"That was some demonstration of kindness this afternoon with all of the gifts, wasn't it?" Grace took a seat on her side of the bed and began taking off her jewelry and placing it on the nightstand. She pinpointed the gifts because that's when Harold's demeanor seemed to have changed.

Harold had already put on a pair of shorts he slept in every night. He peeled off his shirt and climbed under the covers. "It's suspicious. The flag display case for Sophia? A laptop for you? A ham radio for me? A scooter and software for the hipster? How'd Alma do that?"

"It is peculiar, isn't it?"

"More than peculiar, if you ask me."

Grace turned off the lamp on the end table and slipped into bed. A glow from the moon illuminated the room more than she would've expected. They'd decided to not lower the blinds since they were in such a remote place. It seemed like a shame to close themselves off from so much beauty outside.

"What'd you think of the passage Ray read, and then the song Sam and Jennifer performed?" Harold asked. "I had chills."

"I did too," Grace said. "It felt like church. I wanted more."

"Me too."

She could hardly believe her ears. "What do you think is really going on here?"

"What if they're angels?" he whispered.

She hadn't expected that response from Harold, and she'd never heard such reverence in his voice. "Angels?"

"Think about it. They know far too much about us—way more than they should, or possibly could. They only seem to have our best interests at heart. In other words, they don't seem to want anything from us. If anything, they've given us far more than we've given them in the way of cabin rentals."

"Mercy Inn," she whispered.

"And yes, then there's the name of this place."

"We've never talked much about religion," she said. "Do you believe in angels?"

"I do."

"And you really think they can take on human form?"

"Why not?"

"And you think two of them are sitting up there at the lodge right now—and that one of them is a great cook, and the other is a teddy bear of a man who just wants to help people?"

"Who better to represent God?"

The idea thrilled her and frightened her at the same time. It thrilled her because it meant God loved her enough to step into her life. It frightened her because she'd never had much time for church or God.

It wasn't that she was anti-God. She believed he existed, but she'd always had a sneaking suspicion that believing he existed wasn't enough. Suddenly, the many years she'd spent making excuses for not getting active in a church community, coupled with the possibility that she'd spent the last twenty-four hours in the presence of two angels, made her feel quite small.

But if they were angels, shouldn't they make demands of the people they were communicating with? Shouldn't they reveal themselves? Why would they be running an inn in southern Colorado, making fancy coffee, hiring musicians, and giving away expensive Christmas gifts?

"Harold?"

No response.

Apparently, he'd fallen asleep. She had no idea how he could sleep, though, given the possibilities. She wouldn't be doing so anytime soon.

She slipped out of bed, found a Bible in the nightstand, and took it into the bathroom.

* * *

Ray turned over in bed to face Alma. "I think a couple of them are on to us. They seem suspicious."

"What should we do if they press us for answers?"

"Wait for further instructions. But it seems to me that we're going to have to explain who we are at some point."

"Do you realize the ramifications?"

"Not entirely, no."

"It will scare them to death, for starters. And wouldn't that mean we ... wait a minute. This is our final year. Maybe such a revelation is exactly what the Father has in mind."

"You might be right. We should receive more instructions soon." In times like these, Ray was glad he was only a messenger.

Chapter 15

When Harold awoke the next morning, he put his hands behind his head and contemplated his conversation with Grace from the night before. If they really were in the presence of angels, that meant all of the guests *needed* to be in their presence—they needed to hear what they had to say. What had Ray and Alma been saying to him so far?

Ray clearly wasn't happy with the way he and Trey had been getting along. In fact, he even had to play referee between the two of them a couple of times. That wasn't good. Harold could certainly understand why the angels were there for Trey. The boy didn't have a good upbringing, and he seemed a bit lost even now. He needed direction and some good people to care about him. If only he'd lose his arrogant know-it-all attitude, it would make it so much easier to like him.

The truth was, many probably saw Harold as an arrogant know-it-all too. And that had never bothered him until this very moment. If he was really in the presence of angels, they would want him to respect Trey more and maybe even extend mercy and grace toward him.

There was that word again. *Mercy.* In a way, all four of the guests needed mercy. Trey's need was obvious. Sophia seemed to have lost her way and needed some gentle guidance in the right direction. He suspected it was because her identity was wrapped up in her career. Grace ... well, he didn't know what she needed. She'd grown quiet in recent years, dissatisfied with his involvement in politics. Actually, that wasn't really true.

She was dissatisfied with the way politics seemed to have changed him. But how could they not? And why didn't more people care about the decisions their leaders made every day to take away their rights and freedoms? Were they as self-absorbed as he thought or was something else going on with them? Maybe they had grown hopeless? Or were struggling just to put food on the table? Or studying to get into a good college.

He had to admit, up until this point, he really hadn't given people the benefit of the doubt. Maybe his insecurities and lack of empathy for others were the reasons he was here at Mercy Inn. The weight of his foolishness settled in his heart and threatened to overwhelm him.

Grace twitched in her sleep, snapping him out of his self-condemning thoughts. *Ah, Grace.* He watched her sleep for a moment, realizing he hadn't done that in many years. He used to be so taken by her beauty, her compassion, her femininity. How had he ever allowed himself to be pulled away from her—even if only in spirit? And why had she stuck with him all this time? She didn't sign up for the man he'd become.

As soon as she opened her eyes, he leaned over her and kissed her with more passion than they'd known in quite some time. Her lips met his in response, hungry for the affection of her husband.

* * *

115

Grace's head spun as Harold left their bed and headed for the shower. What had gotten into him? But Harold wasn't the only one with a different attitude and outlook.

Last night, she had no idea where to start when she paged through the Bible in the bathroom as Harold slept. She found an index in the back and looked up the word "angel." To her surprise, she found that their description—some had six wings and others had four, and some even had four faces—was nothing like the angel figurines she was accustomed to seeing in Hallmark stores. She also learned that Satan masquerades as an angel of light on occasion, that angels can indeed minister to humans, and sometimes man entertains angels without even knowing it.

That last truth really struck home with her, increasing the likelihood, at least in her mind, that Ray and Alma really were angels. And when she thought about the passage that talked about angels coming to minister to Jesus after he'd been tempted by Satan in the wilderness for forty days, she wondered what that looked like. The Bible didn't go into a lot of detail, but she envisioned angels gathering around him, speaking life-affirming truths to him, and encouraging him in his ministry. Or maybe they just stood next to him as a show of heavenly support as he endured temptation.

If Ray and Alma were angels, they seemed to be doing both for the four guests who were gathered at Mercy Inn this Christmas. One part of her was frightened at the prospect of coming so near to the holy, and another part of her was drawn in. Harold seemed to be, too, if his reverential tone last night was any indication. She could never recall him giving so much respect for anything or anyone.

Fifteen minutes later, he opened the bathroom door. Even

at the age of sixty-three, she still admired his physique. He managed to stay in shape, somehow. That made her self-conscious of her ever-softening midsection.

"Hey beautiful," he said, making her feel a little better about herself.

"Why, Harold Taylor ... are you flirting with me?"

He winked at her.

Her cheeks turned hot and her tummy fluttered.

He turned his back to her and combed his graying hair in the mirror before slipping into a pair of tan khakis and a green polo shirt. "Are you proud of me for remembering to pack a shirt that looks Christmasy?"

"More surprised than anything." She smiled. "I thought about picking out your clothes for you, but figured you'd throw a fit if I selected something you didn't like."

"You're probably right. I would've, but right now, I'm thinking I'd like your input. What do you think?" He spun around like he was a fashion model.

"Like I'm the luckiest woman alive."

Overnight, Harold had gone back to the charmer he had been when they were dating and were first married. She couldn't believe the transformation. The incredible thing was, it didn't feel contrived.

Grace didn't know the first thing about prayer. She'd grown up in a home without any religion. But if she was ever going to start praying, now was the time. *God, I have no idea what I'm doing or if I'm doing this right. You feel more real to me than you ever have. But reading the Bible last night really made me realize how little I actually know about you or any of this stuff. I know that's not really a request, but like I said, I don't know what I'm doing. Will you please continue to lead and guide Harold and me as we learn about you and your ways? Amen.*

She rolled out of bed and took her turn in the shower. This could end up being one of those days a person never forgets. She couldn't wait to get back to the lodge to see what might happen next.

Chapter 16

Sophia finished praying by the side of her bed. She stood, ready to head to the lodge. She still wasn't sure how to broach the subject she needed to discuss with Alma, but she had to know. She wondered if angels had to tell the truth. Ray and Alma had been pretty slick at not answering questions so far, but if she asked Alma point-blank whether or not she was an angel, she'd have to answer the question. Wouldn't she?

Sophia smoothed her red skirt, opting to run a lint brush over her outfit one more time before heading to the lodge. She had gone all out, even putting on a pair of pantyhose, thankful that she'd slipped a pair into her suitcase at the last minute. She couldn't even remember the last time she'd worn a pair. But this was Christmas dinner. And she might just be in the presence of angels. A woman had to look her best.

She glanced over at her dresser where she'd placed the empty flag display box, grateful for the reminder of her father at Christmas. Just as she'd slipped on her coat and was ready to leave, her phone chirped. It was a text from her mom, wishing her a merry Christmas, and of course, asking if she had met any cute, wealthy men. She responded with a Christmas greeting of her own and said she might have found something better than a cute, wealthy man. That would really pique her mother's curiosity.

After she hit send, she saw Anthony's name in her list of messages. He still hadn't sent her a text since she'd left Atlanta, but she hadn't even thought about him in the last twenty-four hours, whereas, on the trip to the inn, she'd checked her phone incessantly. She just needed to forget about him. She swiped left on his thread of texts and hit delete. A sense of satisfaction swept over her. It made her feel like she was finally taking control of something in her personal life for the first time in a while.

She scrolled through her other messages and found a voice mail from Sarah from last night, asking her to call her right away. She hit the return call button.

"Sarah, what did your assistant find out?"

"She's running into the strangest set of circumstances. She started by pulling up the Mercy Inn website, not sure what she was looking for or might find. She didn't find anything out of the ordinary. But my guitar player walked by and asked her why she was staring at a web browser with a 404 error message—you know, the message you see when a website doesn't exist or when you typed in the wrong website address."

"I don't understand." Sophia took a seat in a chair by the door in her cabin.

"I didn't either. Not sure I do now. Megan, my assistant, pointed to her laptop screen and said, 'You don't see a picture of a quaint little inn on the screen?' He glanced at her like she was crazy. 'Um, no. I see a blank screen.'"

"Okay, I still don't understand."

"As other band members and people on my road crew walked by, she asked them what they saw. Every one of them saw nothing but a 404 error message."

"What does that mean?"

"Megan was with me at Mercy Inn two years ago. She interacted with Ray and Alma. If your hunch is right, maybe Megan, you, me—all of us can see the website because we're supposed to see it."

Sophia felt her breath leave her body, and her head started to spin. Could this really be true?

* * *

Harold had forgotten what romance felt like—how it made him feel weak in the knees, almost mimicking the feeling of being drunk. This sudden wave of emotion made the last fifteen years with Grace almost feel like they'd been roommates, rather than husband and wife. And he knew he was completely responsible. He couldn't do anything about the lost years, but he could do something going forward.

Grace opened the bathroom door, wearing only a towel, making it hard for Harold to concentrate.

"I've been thinking about our impending move and I did a little searching for a cabin online," Harold said. "I found one outside of Cortez, which is in the southwest corner of the state, maybe three and a half hours from here."

"Oh?" Grace took a seat at the vanity across the room and began to run a brush through her hair. "How big is the city?"

"Nine thousand people. It has plenty of restaurants and places to shop. I think you'd like a place called Beny's Diner. The photos on social media make the place look incredible. It has a classic diner feel. The food is affordable. And the reviews are great. I can see you writing there a few times a week."

"You little devil. That's what you did when you came back here to our cabin yesterday, isn't it?"

"Guilty as charged. What do you think? Want to take a look at the place online?"

"Yeah, sure. Let me see."

He took a seat on the bench next to her, set the laptop on the vanity, pulled up the website, and began scrolling through the pictures. "This place would be close enough that you could go into town whenever you wanted and close enough for me to open my own handyman business. Then we could retreat to our oasis at night."

Grace began applying her makeup. "I love everything about it. How far outside of Cortez is it?"

"Maybe eleven miles. Is that too far?"

"That's very doable."

"Ray says there's a repeater in the area for the ham radio. So we'd get good reception. Honestly, though, we'd be close enough to the city that we'd be near local services if we ever needed help. I think Ray figured we'd choose something a little more remote, or maybe he was trying to pull a fast one on me by suggesting that we move close to a city with a repeater."

"Why would he do that?"

"So I wouldn't end up so isolated."

"Well, if he did pull a fast one on you, I'll need to shake his hand. Based on the pictures and what you've told me, the place seems ideal."

"I'll see if I can arrange for a viewing as soon as we leave here the day after Christmas. Oh, and I think turnabout is fair play, don't you? Think I'll return the favor with Ray." He smirked, gave her a peck on the cheek, and stood, allowing her to finish getting ready.

* * *

Trey had so many questions. What did Ray and Alma have to gain by giving everybody such expensive gifts? Trust, maybe? But for what reason?

He closed the door to his cabin and headed for the lodge, feeling the need to go into protection mode for the rest of the day. Yesterday, he felt like he was growing closer to everyone in the group—even Harold, to a degree. But after sleeping on yesterday's events, he wasn't going to let his guard down again today. He'd never see these people again. Why should he allow himself to be so vulnerable? He'd be on his way to see Hannah in the morning and probably wouldn't even talk to any of them ever again.

The snow crunched under his feet as he approached the lodge, noticing two squirrels chasing one another up and down several trees—all of which had branches that were lined with a trace of snow. It really was beautiful here. On his hike earlier, he'd taken a few pictures with his phone. He really wanted to take a lot more, but his phone's memory was full, and he didn't trust cloud services to keep his data secure. He made a mental note to trade in his phone for one with a bigger memory on his way to Texas since he was due for an upgrade anyway. If things worked out right, he'd want to take a few photos of Hannah and himself.

He arrived at the lodge at the same time as Harold and Grace. He greeted them and held the door open to let them go in first. As was the case yesterday, he was nearly knocked down by the aroma of bacon, sausage, and coffee when he walked in. He was usually health-conscious, but he had to admit, eating like it was 1965 had its advantages—namely taste, even if it did mean he'd gain a pound or two.

As he filled his plate, he spotted Sophia out of the corner of his eye, seated at a table in the nook that was nearest the window. She didn't have a plate in front of her. She was just sipping some coffee while staring out the window.

He took a seat at her table, reminding himself to not get any closer to her or anybody else. "You look ... distracted. Everything okay?"

"Oh, hey, Trey. Didn't see you come in."

"And you just made my point."

He could see hesitation in her eyes.

"I'm just confused about a lot of things right now." She glanced up at him for a second, and then back down at her coffee mug. She circled the top of the mug with her forefinger before saying anything else. "You heard my story about the pressure my family is putting on me to find somebody to marry."

"That can't be easy." The truth was, he wouldn't mind a little pressure from his parents. Pressure at least meant somebody cared, even if he didn't agree with what they might want for him. But whatever. They had their own lives to live.

Harold and Grace headed for the table next to them. Harold pulled out a chair for Grace, which seemed odd. And they locked eyes as he seated himself. What was going on between them?

"I don't even think that's what really bothering me." Sophia bit her bottom lip, then went all in. "A colleague has been telling me she wants to get involved in Doctors without Borders. The need is so great for basic health care and she says she feels like she could make a real difference that way—unlike her situation right now in which she's bogged down in pushing paperwork between her patients and their insurance companies."

"And you're feeling the pull, too, aren't you?"

"This is going to sound ridiculous, but the flag display box—it finally brought closure to a chapter in my life. Daddy's gone. He's not coming back. Mom is set financially and seems happy in her retirement community. I'm not married and don't really have any prospects. Nothing is tying me to Atlanta anymore."

"What about Greg?"

"I'll admit to wondering about what might have been. But remember how I said we wanted different things?"

"Yeah."

"What he really wanted was a different woman."

Trey shook his head. "He doesn't deserve you."

"Thank you for saying that. I shouldn't have carried a torch for him as long as I have." Sophia pursed her lips. "Maybe he regrets it, and maybe he doesn't. Either way, sometimes you have to come to the conclusion that the past is best left in the past—especially when opportunity is knocking."

He nodded. But it was difficult not to think about the fact that he was about to take a step back into his own past tomorrow.

Chapter 17

As Harold and Grace were finishing their breakfast, Harold waved Ray over to their table. He placed his hand on Grace's across the table and glanced at her, trying to alert her that this was his gotcha moment.

"You already know we want to move to southern Colorado," Harold said to Ray once he arrived. "We're thinking we might even like to find a place close to Mercy Inn. We love this area. It's so beautiful. And it would be nice to know somebody who already lives here. We could pop in and see you and Alma once in a while—maybe even take you out to dinner."

Harold didn't expect Ray to show his cards, assuming he did indeed have something to hide, but he'd get a kick out of watching him perform verbal gymnastics.

Ray raised his eyebrows. "Living in the area would be a fantastic choice. We've loved it here, but we're also thinking this could be our final year here. The four of you might just be Mercy Inn's final four guests."

Harold widened his eyes. "Oh, that's a shame."

Grace set her coffee mug down. "You both seem like you were made for this. Why are you shutting it down, and what will you do next?"

"We'll miss it, no doubt. But the timing just feels right."

Ray scratched his head. "We'll find something else to keep us occupied."

"Will you stay in the area?" Harold asked.

"Alma and I need to have a conversation about what's next for us." Ray spun around in his seat in an apparent attempt to find her.

Grace raised her eyebrows at Harold and he gave her a faint smile.

Ray excused himself.

Harold wiggled his eyebrows. "Wasn't that fun?"

"I don't think you're going to get Ray to crack that easily. He's just not going to come out and say they're angels. In fact, we'll only find out if and when they want us to. But what if we're wrong?"

"I think we both know we aren't."

* * *

Ray cornered Alma in the kitchen and told her about his conversation with Harold and Grace.

Alma opened the oven door to check on something she was cooking. Seeming satisfied that it was done, she grabbed an oven mitt and pulled out a casserole of some sort and set it on the counter. "I don't think it matters all that much, dear, given what we'll be telling everyone soon. We both received the same instructions about how to proceed, right?"

In all these years, Ray had wondered how their guests might respond to finding out that they'd been in the company of angels for Christmas. He sort of envied the angels on the old *Touched by*

An Angel television show. They got to reveal themselves every episode. The bright lights that appeared behind them were a bit over the top, but that was television for you.

"Yes, ma'am. We're on the same page. The timing is going to be difficult though. The gifts really made most of them suspicious yesterday, but maybe in a good way. I mean, maybe it is causing them to contemplate heaven."

"We can handle their questions, dear. We always do." Alma sealed the casserole with foil, then set it in the fridge. "The Father always provides."

* * *

Alma still wondered how the old albums Ray had pulled out came into play. She suspected that this music meant something to all of the guests, and maybe that would set the stage for the revelation. Ray hadn't said anything more about it.

They'd made wonderful progress with their four charges so far. If what Alma had seen this morning was any indication, Harold and Grace were well on their way to rekindling what they'd lost, and Ray had mentioned that Harold seemed less moody this morning. And the fact that Harold was open to living so close to a town was major progress. Sophia appeared to be pondering a big decision this morning, so she was closer to finding the path she was supposed to be on. And Ray and Alma had planted the seed for Trey to open his new graphic design business. Reuniting him with Hannah was part of the plan too.

"Why don't you go gather everybody in the living room, dear. I'll join you in just a few minutes. You can let Sam and Jennifer know we don't really need their services today."

"They were assigned elsewhere this morning. They arranged for a rental car to be delivered to avoid suspicion since their car was incapacitated during the accident. They said their goodbyes a bit ago."

* * *

At Ray's prompting, everyone gathered in the lodge's living room. Trey wondered what kind of surprises they were in for today. Sam and Jennifer had left, which he found odd, especially since it was Christmas day. What better day to listen to Christmas music than today? But it wasn't nearly as odd as when Ray fired up an old record player and began playing a Dean Martin Christmas album.

Wait ... is that? "My parents used to love this album." The album's hissing and scratching brought back memories of Trey's childhood Christmases. Albums were long out of date, even then, but his parents insisted on sticking with them, saying they were the only true way to listen to music. It always made the music sound so dated, in Trey's opinion, but maybe that was part of the charm.

As soon as his feelings of nostalgia passed, it hit him—this was yet another example of something Ray and Alma knew about him that they shouldn't have. This wasn't something he had shared with anybody, ever, including on social media.

The Christmas tree lights changed colors, almost in slow motion, distracting Trey momentarily. And as if on cue, he spotted snowflakes through the window beyond the tree. This really was as close to a perfect Christmas as possible. But perfection didn't really exist. And innkeepers didn't ordinarily take this much interest in their guests. Not that he'd had a lot of experience with innkeepers, but still.

"They don't make 'em like Dean Martin anymore." Harold pointed to the record player over the fireplace. "But what's up with the stack of albums, Ray?"

"I thought it might be enjoyable for all of you to hear some Christmas music from days gone by to get you into the Christmas spirit." Ray waved his hand in the direction of the record player. "I also thought maybe we could sing a few Christmas carols today, if you all are up for it."

That's why Sam and Jennifer are gone.

"We also have one more round of gifts for each of you." Alma rocked back and forth in her chair. "But we'll do it a little differently today. When I call your name, you can go pick a gift from under the tree at random. There aren't any name tags on the ones that are left."

Finally, something that isn't so controlled. It put Trey more at ease. But that still didn't explain the albums—and more specifically, the Dean Martin Christmas album.

He knew very little about the Rat Pack—only what he'd heard from his mother. But hearing Martin's voice now connected him to his past with his parents—when things were simpler. He had to admit, the memories warmed his insides. But those feelings didn't last. His parents had virtually abandoned him. If things were ever going to be made right, they'd need to reach out to him first.

"What's the point of this, Ray?" Trey pointed at the record player. "Somehow, you knew this Dean Martin album had significance to me, so spill."

130

Ray cut his eyes in Alma's direction. Trey followed them and noticed her shake her head, just once, ever so slightly.

"There!" Trey pointed toward Alma, then Ray. "Right there. What's going on?"

"God works in mysterious ways, dear."

"Don't do that—don't quote me platitudes. You're either stalkers, or you're ..." He didn't even believe in angels, so how could he make the accusation?

"What, dear?"

"A-a-angels."

All eyes focused on Ray and Alma.

Instinctively, Trey sat back in his seat, wanting to be as far from them as possible.

"Silver Bells" by Dean Martin played softly in the background.

Sophia, on the other hand, edged forward on the couch—almost like she was hoping they were angels. "I've been wondering the same thing. I know what Hebrews 13:2 says."

"I read that passage last night too," Grace said.

"Will somebody please enlighten me?" Trey raised his eyebrows.

Ray spoke up first. "Do not neglect to show hospitality to strangers, for thereby some have entertained angels unawares."

"I don't get it. I mean, is it possible for people to entertain angels unaware?"

Ray looked at Alma. "It's time."

Chapter 18

Sophia held her breath. Were they really going to confirm her suspicions? If so, she felt like Isaiah when he came into contact with angels—unworthy, unclean.

Ray got up and put a different album on the record player. "Silent Night," the first song on Mariah Carey's Christmas album, began to play.

"Hey, this was one of my favorite Christmas albums when I was in high school," Sophia said. "My friends and I used to love this. My favorite song on this album was 'Miss You Most.' This really brings back memories."

"Nothing like a little teenage angst, right, dear?"

Sophia nodded and glanced at the ceiling, recalling her best friends sitting on her bed while listening to the song and going on and on about their latest crush.

"Not to be rude, but you were just about to reveal something to us," Harold said.

"Oh, right," Ray said.

Ray and Alma stood and joined hands.

Sophia's stomach churned. The suspense was killing her.

"Ray and I have been leading Christmas celebrations like this for many, many years ... seventy-one, to be precise." Alma looked up into Ray's eyes.

Sophia gasped. "How is that possible? You'd have to be ninety years old. Maybe older. And neither of you look ..." She was pretty sure she knew what they were going to say, but she had to hear the words.

"We're angels, sent here by the Father to show people mercy in ways they probably never understood they needed," Alma said.

Silence.

Sophia knew God through his only begotten son, Jesus Christ. She believed in the Bible and everything it said—including the parts about angels. She just never expected to be in the presence of one, or two, in this case. She had no idea how to respond or what to do. Apparently, nobody else did either.

Heaven decided to come down to visit them. How could they do anything but feel overwhelmingly grateful and maybe a little frightened?

"And Sam and Jennifer?" Sophia asked.

Ray nodded. "They are angels too."

Sophia heard gasps all around the room.

"Every year, the Father chooses the guests he wants to show up at Mercy Inn for Christmas," Alma said. "Only they, and previous guests, can see Mercy Inn, or anything to do with us—including our website, our phone number, or our email address."

Sophia's conversation with Sarah ran through her mind. Then it hit her. Sarah's band hadn't been able to see the inn's website that her assistant had brought up. Everything Alma was saying was true. Sophia just knew it, and she began to tremble. The moment was nearly too much for her to bear. "That explains a lot." She dabbed at the tears that were forming in the corners of her eyes.

"I'm not sure I want to admit it, but I have to say, I think I believe you," Trey said.

"Why us?" Sarah stretched out her hands, palms to the sky. "Why reveal yourselves to us? You could've avoided this if you hadn't given us those gifts. I mean, they were so specific."

"I suspect that the four of you needed such a special revelation from heaven," Ray said. "But I can't say for sure. We're simply messengers. The Father speaks, and we obey. We found out last Christmas that this would be our final year at Mercy Inn. But that was all we knew then."

Alma nodded. "And before you got here, the only thing I knew was that I was supposed to go buy the gifts."

"How did you know what to buy?"

"We can't reveal everything, dear, but the Father provided all the information I needed before I even knew your names."

"Incredible," Harold said.

"And the albums?" Sophia asked.

"Same thing," Ray said. "After all of you arrived, I received instructions to pull these albums out of my old collection. I didn't know why. I simply obeyed."

"Do you know why now?" Trey asked.

"I really don't. But we'll find out more as the afternoon wears on."

"Miss You Most" began playing and Sophia closed her eyes and sang along. The moment was nearly overwhelming, but she just went with it. What other choice did she have?

* * *

Grace felt oddly at peace—not at all fearful like she thought she might. If God cared enough to get involved in human affairs, especially her affairs, then she couldn't imagine a better Christmas.

"So, for seventy-one years, you've been ministering to people like us, helping us do ... what?" Sophia asked.

"Every charge is different," Alma said. "But in nearly every circumstance, it was to either help them heal from a past hurt or to make a difficult decision about the future. Mostly, I think Ray and I are just here to listen."

"So you show them compassion and mercy, and that helps them get back on track?" Grace asked.

"That's a good way to put it, dear."

The angels sat back down.

"Is it okay for us to ask what you're supposed to help us with individually?" Grace asked.

"You may ask anything, but some things are better left for you to figure out on your own," Ray said. "Typically, we ask you questions that will prompt you to do the work that needs to be done."

Grace felt so inadequate, and yet so loved. She'd spent the majority of her life living in fear and just going along to get along. So much of what she'd done felt meaningless. She realized that now. But her newfound passion for writing gave her more purpose than she'd had in years. Maybe it was because her deepest desire was for her words to mean something to readers.

"I think you've already done that in my case," Grace said. "Clearly, my teaching and librarian background prepared me to write. And your gift will spur me on to pursue it like never before."

"Ray and I couldn't be happier, dear." Alma had such warmth in her eyes.

Ray got up and put on a Christmas album by Andy Williams from 1965. "For this next selection, I'm going to start with the second side."

As soon as Grace heard Williams' version of "The First Noel," she knew why Ray chose it—why he'd received instruction from on high to play it first.

"This song ..." Grace tried not to get emotional. "During my sophomore year in college, I came home for Christmas and my dad played the album nonstop for days. I was intrigued and awed by this particular song about the birth of the Savior, even though I knew very little about him. Now it feels like I've come full circle."

"That's beautiful, dear. And we couldn't be happier."

"Are we allowed to tell anybody that we spent the Christmas holiday with angels—about what happened here?" Trey said.

"Certainly," Ray said. "But you should know that most won't believe you."

* * *

In light of what Ray said, Sophia considered her work colleagues—many of whom didn't respect people of faith. That wasn't the case with all of them, but quite a few were all about science, and joints and muscles, and things they could see. Most, if they were honest, admitted that when patients prayed, they healed faster, but they chalked that up to the power of the mind. If she were to come home and tell them about her encounter with two angels who appeared as an elderly couple, she'd never have credibility with them again. She might even lose future referrals.

Her personal relationships wouldn't go much better. Her mother had no place for God or religion in her life. Her sister didn't seem all that interested, either. And the few friends she had outside of work would never understand what she was talking about. It was a miracle, of sorts, that she possessed any faith. But she'd attended a Jesuit university and most of the students there were accustomed to attending church services every Sunday. Some even went every morning. When a new friend on campus had invited her one day, she went and she'd never stopped going.

Hearing about and finally fully understanding that Jesus died for her sins, drew her in. She started attending a small group Bible study on Wednesday nights with her friend and began to understand the various doctrines of the church for the first time. They added stability to her life—something she could count on. And her prayer life sprang to life out of her gratitude for what Christ had done for her.

Since her college days, her faith had only grown stronger, but she had to admit to herself that she was too timid in matters of faith around her family and colleagues. But this trip would change that, no matter the cost. She'd come face to face with two angels. How could she not be different?

Chapter 19

Harold rubbed the back of his neck. This was all a bit much to take in—even if he had suspected it. He had so many questions, but the answers almost didn't matter. He was sitting in front of two angels who'd been sent from heaven to guide them. Asking them about whether they took on other forms, or if they slept, or about their next assignment seemed so petty in light of the reasons they were sent to this group of people. And it called into question Harold's way of life. He'd never made any time for God. Why would God make time for him?

Snowball jumped into Harold's lap, pranced around in a few circles, and finally plopped down. It felt so odd, yet so invigorating to be in touch with the spiritual and the physical world at the same time. He'd never felt more alive.

Ray put the next album on and Harold knew it instantly. The song was "There Were Three Ships." The album was *Christmas Day in the Morning* by Burl Ives. His grandmother used to play it when he was young. He'd picked up a copy of it after marrying Grace and she grew to love it as much as he did. This album could've been chosen just as much for Grace as it was for him, and he voiced that sentiment.

"The two of you are seen as one in heaven, dear," Alma said.

He reached over and grabbed Grace's hand.

Everybody seemed content to sit in silence, listening to Ives. "What Child Is This?" was especially compelling, given that they now had some experience with sitting in the presence of angels. The song took on a much deeper meaning for Harold than it ever had before.

The invisible had become visible. The theoretical had become reality. The spiritual world had come to the physical world. How could anything ever be the same after that? How could he hold contempt for Trey and his generation, even though he vehemently disagreed with the way they viewed the world? How could he want to withdraw from people when God had seen fit to send ministering angels to him, even in his ugly condition?

"Trey, I need to ask for your forgiveness," Harold said. "We grew up with very different ways of looking at life, and while I don't understand yours, that doesn't give me the right to treat you the way I have. Will you forgive me?"

All eyes turned to Trey.

"Only if you'll forgive me." Trey's eyes softened. "Just as you've viewed me as a young punk, I've viewed you as an out-of-touch old man. We do have big differences, but maybe we can learn from each other instead of dissing one another?"

Both men got up and shook hands. Trey leaned in for an apparent hug, but Harold pulled back. There was no need to go that far.

"Deal," Harold said. "And if Grace and I can help you in any way to get your graphic design business up and running, call us. I know a little about starting my own business. And Grace here, she knows a lot about everything."

They took their seats as "Down in Yon Forest" played on the turntable. Ives didn't have a particularly good voice in Harold's opinion, but it was distinctive. Maybe that's how he secured a record contract. Even so, his Christmas music had a reverential tone that Harold hadn't picked up on before.

When the song was over, Harold scratched his head. "Now what do we do?"

"We expected more questions from all of you," Ray said. "Feel free to ask us what you're thinking."

* * *

Trey had never really been much for religion. But he certainly wasn't going to deny the existence of angels after everything he'd experienced over the past two days. And the reconciliation he'd just experienced with Harold was nothing short of incredible. But why him? Why was he selected from the millions of people on earth to witness this?

He could understand them showing up for Sophia and Grace since they seemed to believe in God. But maybe that wasn't it. Maybe it was based more on need. The four of them were headed in one direction before they arrived at Mercy Inn, based on certain beliefs that held them back, and they needed a push in a new direction. But did God really care about such things?

"Okay, here's my question. Actually, I have a series of questions, if you don't mind." Trey looked at Ray and Alma.

"Of course not, dear."

"Why us? Why the other hundreds of people you have ministered to over the years here? What about the millions of others who are struggling with addictions, or on the verge of leaving their spouses, or are dying with cancer? What about the world leaders who need to be pushed in a different direction? Their decisions affect so many people. What about the dictators who need to be confronted to choose good over evil? I mean ... why pick a retired plumber, a retired librarian, a family practice doctor, and a graphic artist?"

The room grew tense for a moment, and Trey was satisfied with himself for asking the tough questions—the same way a reporter might be. He sat back in his chair and waited for heaven to speak. He believed it owed him an answer.

Ray locked eyes with Trey, causing a shiver to run down his spine. "What makes you think you're the only charges and we're the only angels, son? What makes you think other angels aren't working as addiction counselors, marriage counselors, and oncologists? What makes you think we don't visit and pray for the terminally ill in hospitals and nursing facilities around the world? What makes you think we don't visit every governmental agency in the world—whispering truth into the ears of leaders? What makes you think we don't stand at the ready to defeat evil in all forms?"

Trey's eyes shifted from one person to the next until he'd come full circle, back to Ray. "I'd never considered it. Are you saying all of those examples are true?"

"I'm saying you can't contain heaven, and you can't quantify it. God does what he wills. But rest assured, he hears the pleas of those who are suffering. He knows every dictator, every terrorist, and every oppressor by name. He also knows and hears every victim who calls out to him. And he knows the name of every sick person who cries out to him. The world looks chaotic, but never mistake that for God not showing up. He is ever-present and ever-ready. He cares about the largest catastrophe and the smallest hurt."

"So why does he allow so much evil?"

Ray stood to retrieve a Bible from the mantle above the fireplace. Once he'd done so, he took his seat. "I'm going to let the Lord himself answer this for you. Are you familiar with the story of Job?"

"The guy who lost everything for no apparent reason?"

"Surely, that was his attitude at first, Trey. And that led him to question why God allowed him to lose it all. I'm going to jump around a bit to give you a small taste of what the Lord said in response."

Then the LORD answered Job out of the whirlwind and said:

"Who is this that darkens counsel by words without knowledge? Dress for action like a man; I will question you, and you make it known to me.

"Where were you when I laid the foundation of the earth? Tell me, if you have understanding. Who determined its measurements—surely you know! Or who stretched the line upon it? On what were its bases sunk, or who laid its cornerstone, when the morning stars sang together and all the sons of God shouted for joy?

"Or who shut in the sea with doors when it burst out from the womb, when I made clouds its garment and thick darkness its swaddling band, and prescribed limits for it and set bars and doors, and said, 'Thus far shall you come, and no farther, and here shall your proud waves be stayed'?

"Have you commanded the morning since your days began, and caused the dawn to know its place, that it might take hold of the skirts of the earth, and the wicked be shaken out of it? It is changed like clay under the seal, and its features stand out like a garment. From the wicked their light is withheld, and their uplifted arm is broken."

Then the LORD answered Job out of the whirlwind and said:

"Dress for action like a man; I will question you, and you make it known to me. Will you even put me in the wrong? Will you condemn me that you may be in the right? Have you an arm like God, and can you thunder with a voice like his?

"Adorn yourself with majesty and dignity; clothe yourself with glory and splendor. Pour out the overflowings of your anger, and look on everyone who is proud and abase him. Look on everyone who is proud and bring him low and tread down the wicked where they stand. Hide them all in the dust together; bind their faces in the world below. Then will I also acknowledge to you that your own right hand can save you."

Ray glanced up. "Shall I continue?"

Trey hung his head and held up his hand. He had nothing to say after that. His face was hot with shame. God was far more involved than he'd ever imagined. It made him feel both small and big at the same time.

Nobody moved or said anything for what felt like an hour to Trey, but in reality, was probably only fifteen or twenty seconds.

Ray finally stood and approached the stereo on the mantle. He selected a CD, not an album, which Trey found odd—unless the music Ray was about to play hadn't come out on vinyl.

Rhianna's voice filled the air. Trey knew the song instantly: "A Child is Born" off the *Now That's What I Call Christmas!* 4 album. It was a compilation of many modern artists, including Sheryl Crow, Darius Rucker, Christina Aguilera, and Colbie Caillat. He'd downloaded it when it first came out maybe seven years ago. It'd become his favorite Christmas album. So, of course, Ray would know about it.

Trey gave Ray a knowing nod.

Chapter 20

They broke for lunch, and Sophia was grateful to get a chance to think about what had just taken place. For the first time, all four charges were gathered at one table to eat. They were unified unlike anything Sophia thought was possible just two days ago. But when heaven shows up, you pay attention.

The music from the record player continued throughout their Christmas meal which included ham, mashed potatoes, biscuits, and fresh green beans. And Alma had made a casserole that included bacon, sausage, hash browns, eggs, and a few other ingredients that made it taste out of this world. Sophia giggled at the thought.

The four charges chit-chatted throughout lunch and gathered back in the living room afterward, where Ray directed everyone.

"Shall we continue our game of Nicebreaker?" Ray said.

Everybody nodded their approval.

"Don't feel like you have to give a different answer just because you know our true identities," Ray said. "We're not expecting perfection from you. This game has always been about helping charges process the challenges they're facing, and sometimes that's messy."

That made Sophia feel better. She'd already been contemplating how she might answer differently, given what she knew about them. She would be as honest as possible, which already felt like a hedge.

"Let's start with Alma."

"Okay, dear. This question is for Sophia." She flipped a card from her stack. "What is your favorite work experience, and why?"

"Before she answers, can I ask a question?" Trey held his finger in the air. "Do the two of you know the question you're pulling out of the stack before you even do it. And if you do, then are you pulling out questions that we need to work through?"

"We have the power to know, but we don't use it," Ray said. "Alma and I have always operated as humans might while interacting with humans during our assignment at Mercy Inn. Those were the instructions we received the first year we were here."

"Good to know," Trey said. "Sophia?"

"My favorite work experience ... and why? Hmm." Sophia looked at the ceiling as she searched her memories. "My employer encourages us to volunteer our medical services once a month at one of the several free clinics in the poorer parts of town."

"That sounds like a wonderful service, dear."

"I thought so too. The Saturday before I left for this trip, I went to one of those clinics, and a woman brought in her niece. I can't disclose the girl's real name, but I'll call her Camila. The little girl was four years old. She had no medical records in the system, other than her birth. According to her aunt, she had never even been to a doctor or dentist to her knowledge.

"It hit me hard. Here was a little girl who lives in the wealthiest country in the world, but she wasn't receiving proper medical care. Her parents were no longer in the picture. They were dealing with their own issues, so they signed over their parental rights to Camila's aunt."

"What did her aunt bring her in for, dear?"

"She read about the free clinic in the newspaper and thought she should bring Camila in because she'd been complaining about headaches. I ordered a CT scan and found a brain tumor. She needed immediate surgery. Her aunt filed for medical assistance with the state, but approval can take weeks or even months.

"What did you do?" Grace asked.

"I found a colleague who agreed to do the surgery for free—it was the same colleague who'd been talking to me about Doctors without Borders. She's out of town on a mission, but she'll be back day after tomorrow. The surgery is scheduled for the following day. I'd appreciate all of your prayers for Camila."

* * *

Ray led the group in a prayer for Camila. Grace never felt more alive. Praying with an angel? What a privilege. When Ray finished, Grace had a question for Sophia—well, it was more a statement.

"It seems like you've got your own Doctors without Borders right there in Atlanta. I'm not discouraging you from going overseas because from what I've heard, that organization does great work. But have you considered opening a surgical center in Atlanta that would pull from a team of doctors who would be willing to perform surgeries for those who cannot afford to pay for them?"

"I did toy with the idea at one point, actually," Sophia said. "But it just seems impossible. Funding such an operation would be a huge undertaking. I wouldn't even know where to start."

"I might be able to help with that," Trey said. "My company specializes in creating websites, social media campaigns, and crowd-funding campaigns for projects like this. And like you, we're encouraged to be on the lookout for cases like yours so we can volunteer to help. Not only do we set up everything for you, but we already have established contacts with potential donors in many industries who trust our vetting process."

"That sounds perfect, Trey!" Sophia got up and hugged him. He never even had a chance to get up from his seat.

"Okay, then. We can talk more about it later. I'm happy to help."

"Well, that's exciting," Ray said. "I have a feeling that the funding for such a wonderful place will materialize if it's supposed to. Let's pray about it right now."

They bowed their heads, and Ray began. "Father, you know that the needs are great in Atlanta for the type of facility that is on Sophia's heart—one that will minister to the least of these. We ask that you would provide the funding if it's your will. And if it is, may this surgical center be a testament to your mercy and grace for many years to come."

"Amen," the group said in unison.

"Trey, you're up next," Ray said.

"I'll go with Grace." Trey chose a card and flipped it over. "What was, or is, one of your family's craziest beliefs or con-spiracy theories?"

Harold smiled. "You can be honest. I already know it'll be about me."

The room chuckled. But the last thing she wanted to do was make Harold feel like she was picking on him after he'd made so much progress over the past couple of days. She'd ease her way into her answer.

"First, don't all of us have some sort of conspiracy theory?" Grace asked. "I have several of my own that come to mind. I'm convinced that supermarkets put the milk in the back of the store so I'll have to pass dozens of other products on the way to retrieving the only item I went in to buy. I mean, who just goes in and only buys milk, right?"

"I think your conspiracy theory is correct," Trey said. "I heard an economist and a food writer on NPR a few years ago talking about this. They didn't claim to be experts and said they didn't have any inside knowledge. Even so, one of them pointed out that bread is also a staple but stores often place it far away from the milk. He believed it was done to force customers to cover more ground, which means they'll pass even more products on the way to finding it."

"I knew it!" Grace poked her finger in the air, lightening the mood but delaying the inevitable. "Well ... as you might imagine, Harold has a conspiracy theory or two, as well." She nudged him with her elbow. She had made fun of herself. Hopefully, he could take a little ribbing now too.

"Remember the NSA scandal about them monitoring Americans' cell phones without authorization? When that story first broke, Harold was convinced he was on some watch list based on political conversations he had over the years on his cell phone. So he ditched his smartphone in favor of a phone that he believed couldn't be tracked."

"Guilty." Harold raised his hand, and then pulled his phone out of his pocket. "This is an MVNO phone, and generally speaking, these aren't tracked. Some people call them burner phones."

"I'll bite ... what does MVNO stand for?" Trey asked.

"Mobile Virtual Network Operator," Harold said. "They usually do not have their own network infrastructure and licensed radio spectrum. As long as they do not, they are not tracked. But you have to be careful, because some, in fact, do have their own network. If you choose the kind with a SIM card though, you're safe. You can always ditch the SIM card and buy a new one. I do so every month."

"I had no idea," Trey said.

Harold nodded. "Also, these prepaid phones are so cheap that you can toss them in the trash every so often and buy a new one for less than fifty dollars."

"I know who I'm calling during Armageddon," Trey said.

"I doubt it," Harold said. "I'll have changed my number one hundred and eighteen times by then."

The room erupted in laughter.

This went so much better than Grace thought it would. Harold was talking about some of his fears without any reservation and without taking offense—neither of which he'd have done two days ago.

Chapter 21

"Okay, enough about my conspiracy theories," Harold said. "Whose turn is it to ask the next question?"

"I believe it's Grace's turn," Ray said.

"I choose Alma." Grace flipped a card. "How did you meet the love of your life?"

Alma contemplated the question. She could only reveal so much information, but she also wanted to be as true to the spirit of the game as possible, especially given how honest everybody had been so far with their own difficult answers.

She reached over and grabbed Ray's hand. "As you probably know, angels are created beings—we're not human. We can take on the shape of a human, though, and that's where it can be a bit confusing for humans." She paused.

"Does that mean you're incapable of love?" Sophia asked.

"It means we're messengers who have been set apart by God to do with as he pleases. But to answer your question, since we're not human, we don't have all of the same capabilities—at least in any sense you can relate to."

"So you and Ray aren't really in love, then?" Sophia said.

"Well, yes and no, dear." Alma paused again to give them time to process all of this information before determining that she should just answer the question before even more questions arise.

"It's complicated," Alma said. "Let me start at the beginning. In 1946, we were assigned to the Christmas Eve service at Community Bible Church. It used to be located just up the road a few miles. Ray took on the appearance of a teenage boy, and I was a giggly teenage girl who was allowed to join the choir at the last minute to sing several traditional Christmas carols."

Ray spoke up. "I couldn't take my eyes off the girl in the middle of the back row."

Alma giggled. "After the service, he approached me and told me I was pretty."

"It really was awkward," Ray said. "It gave me a glimpse into what humans have to deal with when it comes to relationships."

"That's so sweet," Sophia said. "So, you felt all the butterflies a human would in a situation like that?"

"Like Alma said, it's complicated," Ray said. "I can't go into any more detail. But the following Christmas, we were assigned as an elderly couple to run Mercy Inn. Neither of us has aged in appearance since."

Alma studied their faces. Sophia and Grace seemed quite accepting of the limited amount of information Ray and Alma had shared. The slight frown on Trey's face told her he wanted to know more. And Harold's face was expressionless as his eyes shifted from one person to the next. Alma couldn't get a feel for what he might be thinking.

"I'm still having a difficult time digesting this," Trey said. "I know it's true. I can feel it. We've been given a glimpse of the supernatural, but there are so many unanswered questions."

"Like what, dear?"

"Like, what happens after we die? Does everyone go to heaven? What does heaven look like? Can we see what is happening here on earth from heaven? What will we do in heaven? Are animals there? Are angels there? Will we remember our friends, families? If so, how will we interact with them? Will we see Jesus face to face?"

"You weren't kidding, dear. That is a lot of questions. Do you want to take this one, Ray?"

He nodded. "The answer to some of those questions can be found in the Bible. The answer to a couple of them cannot be revealed while you're still here on earth. And as for seeing Jesus face to face—I can answer that one. If you've placed your faith in him, you will indeed see him. He ascended into heaven to prepare a place for all those who would believe."

"What kind of place?" Trey said.

"A glorious one."

Alma studied the looks on the faces around the room. They still wanted more, but Ray and Alma weren't authorized to tell them more. "When you get home, begin to read your Bibles—many of the answers to your questions can be found there."

For him who has ears to hear, let him hear.

* * *

Ray indicated that it was Sophia's turn. She chose Ray. He and Alma were often left out of the early rounds, but now that everybody knew their true identity, they were quite popular. That was okay. They had questions, naturally.

Sophia flipped a card. "What makes you laugh?"

"Corny jokes—the cornier the better," Ray said.

"Boy, that's the truth," Alma said.

"Also, the sight of children playing."

"Does that mean you get away from the inn sometimes?" Sophia asked. "I mean, are you here year-round or ... ?"

"We do go into town when the situation warrants it, dear. But we're only here during Christmas—for a few days. As soon as our charges leave, the place vanishes. Nobody even knows it was here."

"So where do you go the rest of the year?" Sophia said.

"That's not a question we can answer," Ray said. "But we stay quite busy. It also means I have access to many other opportunities to laugh though. I laugh when I see families playing board games and acting goofy. I giggle like a school girl when I see children interacting with pets. And this might surprise you, but I'm always on the lookout for good comedy on television."

"Were you a Letterman or a Leno guy back in the day?" Harold asked.

"I'll never tell. It would make it sound as if heaven were taking sides."

The room erupted in laughter, and that seemed to ease the tension. Their charges had received quite a shock today and they seemed to be on edge—not knowing what was going to happen next, or what would be expected of them. Ray could certainly understand their apprehension.

"Well, we promised you more gifts," Alma said. "This would be a good time to open them. Then maybe everyone can take some time to themselves and reflect on everything that's happened here. Maybe go back to your rooms for a while to call relatives or friends to wish them a merry Christmas."

Alma called their names one by one and they selected a gift of their choosing from under the tree, taking their time to open and display each one. Sophia was delighted to end up with a pair of mittens Alma had knitted. Grace smiled when she opened a package of gourmet coffee beans. Harold nodded when he opened his gift and saw a pair of headphones. And Trey must've been happy with the video game he received because he was already immersed in reading the description on the back of the packaging.

"Of course, feel free to trade gifts if you want to," Alma said. "Once you're done, it's time for a break. We'll see you back here in a couple of hours for dinner."

* * *

Ray peeked out the door from the kitchen when he heard the soft hum of conversation coming from the nook. He hoped that they'd all had time to process everything during their free time. The good news was, all four charges were chatting in a circle. So much had changed over the course of the last few days. Ray took a few seconds to bow his head and thank the Father for the work he had done.

A few minutes later, Ray and Alma headed for the nook with the first round of food. Ray carried a platter with the biggest turkey he'd ever seen. And the smell was heavenly, if he did say so himself.

"If you'll all take your seats," Alma said, "we'll have the rest of food on the table lickety-split, as Ray might say."

Sophia and Grace helped with the remaining dishes. After they finished, Sophia pulled Ray aside, biting her lip before saying what she had to say. "I know you're here to help guide us in a certain direction, but I'm still confused about that. I've been thinking more about the surgical center idea, but I just can't imagine how I'll ever fund it—even with Trey's marketing help."

Ray put a hand on her shoulder. "So you're considering Doctors without Borders instead?"

She nodded.

"You have two noble choices in front of you. I can't make that decision for you, but I assure you that God isn't keeping this information from you. He just wants you to ask him, and then trust him. He'll take care of the details after that."

"How will I know?"

"The circumstances will have his fingerprints all over them."

"So I should relax then?"

"*Pursue* would be the word I'd use. Pursue God. Pursue his will. Then trust him to reveal it."

She smiled. "Do you think I'll find out before I leave tomorrow morning?"

"You never know."

Sophia's phone chirped. She glanced down at it.

"Anything important?"

"My office has news about one of my patients. He had a heart attack a couple of days ago and has just passed away."

"I'm truly sorry to hear that."

"Thanks. I need to make a couple of calls."

"Of course. Take your time."

Sophia disappeared out the front door.

She would find the answer to her future in that phone call. Ray was sure of it.

Chapter 22

Harold took a seat at a table in the nook, expecting Grace to follow, but she excused herself and stepped outside for some reason—maybe to check on Sophia. Trey sat down at Harold's table and began to eat. Maybe the two of them could be friendly after everything they had learned about one another the last couple of days. It was Christmas after all.

"I get the feeling that we're supposed to take something away from this," Trey said. "Don't you? Like we're supposed to take what we've learned and do something important with it."

Harold nodded, took a bite of his turkey, and swallowed it. "This experience has certainly shaped my future."

"How so?"

"Grace and I went from planning on buying a secluded cabin to buying one closer to a local community. And personally, I went from wanting to be isolated to wanting to be involved in that community."

"That is quite a difference." Trey nodded.

"Are you going to follow through and open your own graphic design business?"

"Do you think that's enough, based on what everybody else seems to be planning?"

"I don't know if that's the right way to measure it. I took a walk during our break and it gave me some time to think. Seems to me that all of us needed a course correction. Everything I've heard indicates that you're supposed to open your own business. I wouldn't underestimate the importance of that. It could provide for you and your family one day."

"Good point."

They sat in silence for a few seconds.

"Hey, do you think we'll ever see Ray and Alma again?" Trey asked.

"I hope so."

Grace and Sophia came back inside, arm and arm. They must've had a girl moment. This trip was full of surprises. Harold almost felt bad for spending Christmas in the company of angels. Most people would never knowingly have such an opportunity. Then he remembered what Ray said to Trey about the possibility of angels being everywhere, in every circumstance. And that warmed his heart.

Something else had occurred to Harold during his walk. After he opened his handyman business, he was going to offer his services to widows and the disabled for free. Maybe he'd contact a church once they got settled somewhere and work through a pastor to find such people to help. Maybe he'd even begin worshiping there with Grace.

As much as he was still hoping to be able to call Ray from time to time, he got the overwhelming sense that everything was going to be just fine if he couldn't.

Grace and Sophia joined them at the table. They both had tears in their eyes—good tears; he could tell. "So, is anybody going to fill us in? What's going on?"

"One of my patients passed away a few minutes ago." Sophia

took a seat at the table. "He suffered a massive heart attack recently. He was just forty-seven years old." She paused. "He never married. He had one sibling—a brother—who works in Europe somewhere. A nurse just told me he tried to get back in time to say goodbye, but he didn't make it."

"So he died all alone?" Harold said.

"I'm not sure whether his parents are still alive or not. He never mentioned anybody besides his brother in his family." Sophia paused again to collect herself.

"There's more to the story." Grace rubbed Sophia's shoulder.

Sophia shook her head. "He told a nurse that he knew about my work among the less fortunate in the community at the various free clinics I'd volunteered in. So, a couple of years ago, he instructed his attorney to draw up the paperwork to place his entire estate, which was worth millions, in a fund that would pay for the cost of a medical clinic for the less fortunate. And he wanted me to be its director." She put her hand over her mouth, not even trying to conceal her tears. "I think I have the answer to my prayer."

* * *

Trey had never been one to show emotion, but his eyes grew misty when he heard Sophia's news. She seemed like the sort of person who deserved such a break.

Sophia reached out and touched Trey's arm. "If, and I do say if, all of this works out, can I be your first paying client? I know you offered to volunteer your services to raise funds and awareness through your current employer, but with the initial funding coming through, I'll gladly pay you if you have your own company up and running. I'll need good talent to help get the word out."

"That's very gracious. Thank you."

"Of course." Sophia stood. "I really do feel like I need to get back to Atlanta right away though to meet my patient's brother. He's going to want to talk to me. And I need to make sure there are no hard feelings over his brother leaving everything for my clinic."

She hugged Harold and Grace, then Trey. After she pulled away, she took out her business card, wrote her cell phone number on the back, and slipped it into Trey's hand. "Call me." She stopped briefly at the checkout counter and apparently filled in Ray and Alma. They came around the other side and offered her a hug.

Trey offered to help Sophia pack her rental car, but she said she only had one suitcase. "Are you sure you need to go tonight? It's quite a drive to their airport in Colorado Springs."

"I really need to get home. And I have a feeling that our friends will put in a good word with their other angel friends to keep me safe." She nodded toward Ray and Alma.

"Okay, be safe. And I'll be in touch." He flicked her business card.

* * *

The next morning, the three remaining charges met in the lodge to say their goodbyes. Alma handed each of them a bagged lunch for the road. Feelings of nostalgia swept over Ray as he looked around the old inn one last time.

Their work here was done and everybody was ready to return to their routines, if that was even possible. Actually, they would have new routines. He'd already placed a call to a realtor in Cortez and she said she'd be waiting for the Taylors to show them the place they were interested in.

"We can't thank you and Alma enough for everything you did for us," Grace said.

"We were happy to do it, dear."

Trey was the next one to offer his thanks. "Ray and Alma, you've given me hope. Saying 'thank you' just doesn't feel like enough, but I don't know what else to say. So, thank you."

"We're so happy for you, dear. But we were just the messengers. God loves you. In fact, he loves you so much that he sent his only son to die for your redemption."

"That sounds more true to me now than it ever has."

"That's because it is, dear."

"I believe you."

Those words caused Ray's heart to flutter as Alma patted her hands.

"It's hard not to believe after what we've encountered the past few days," Harold said.

The group shared one final hug, and a reverential silence fell over Mercy Inn. The three charges pulled away and headed for their vehicles. They almost seemed hesitant to leave. Ray considered that to be a testament to the bond they'd formed at this special place, mixed with uncertainty about the future. And maybe, just maybe, they had developed a small attachment to Ray and Alma.

Even so, their work here was done. Ray and Alma joined hands and watched the cars pull out of the lot. They waved until everyone was out of sight. The wind picked up and a light snow began to fall just as the inn, and the angels, vanished.

Other Titles by Lee Warren

In This Series

Mercy Inn: A Christmas Novella (The Mercy Inn Series, Book 1)

Comeback: A Mercy Inn Series Short Story

The Reunion: A Christmas Novella (The Mercy Inn Series, Book 2)

The Revelation: A Christmas Novella (The Mercy Inn Series, Book 3)

Devotionals and Gift Books

Single Servings: 90 Devotions to Feed Your Soul

Fun Facts for Sports Lovers

Inspiring Thoughts for Golfers

Racing for Christ: 50 Devotions for NASCAR Fans

Experiencing Christmas: A 31-Day Family Christmas Devotional

Finishing Well: Living with the End in Mind (A Devotional)

Flying Solo: 30 Devotions to Encourage the Never-Married

Essays

Common Grounds: Contemplations, Confessions, and (Unexpected) Connections from the Coffee Shop

Sacred Grounds: First Loves, First Experiences, and First Favorites

Higher Grounds: When God Steps into the Here and Now

Finding Common Ground: Boxed Set (Books 1-3)

Writing

Write That Devotional Book: From Dream to Reality

Write That Book in 30 Days: Daily Inspirational Readings

You can find out more about Lee Warren's books here:
http://www.leewarren.info/books

Subscribe to Lee's weekly email list (dedicated to slowing down and living deeper), and you'll receive a digital freebie as a thank you. You will also receive notifications about his newest books and become eligible for random giveaways. Sign up here: http://www.leewarren.info/email-list

Follow Lee on social media:
https://www.facebook.com/leewarrenauthor
https://twitter.com/leewarren

Visit Lee's website:

http://www.leewarren.info

CPSIA information can be obtained
at www.ICGtesting.com
Printed in the USA
LVHW041743301022
731931LV00009B/708

9 781730 963681